# YULETIDE HORRORS

## Volume 1

I0456322

## Christofer Nigro

### with Dustin Dreyling

### Cover design & formatting:
### Elden Ardiente of Lungga Creatives

# DEDICATIONS

This book is dedicated, first and foremost, to the memory of my beloved grandmother Gertrude "Trudie" Nigro, who loved the holidays, particularly Christmas, and was also a fan of the horror genre. I hope to proudly carry on the legacy she left the family as best I can.

This book is further dedicated to every fellow miscreant out there who believes the holidays are worth acknowledging and celebrating for their cultural, psychological, and spiritual importance; that the horror genre is a worthy one to read and write for its own creative, sociological, and psychological importance to the human psyche – and that mashing the two together could be as appealing to the aesthetic and philosophical palate as mixing peanut butter and jelly can be to the one dedicated to taste of a more physical sort.

Very special thanks to my colleagues, friends, and editors Dustin Dreyling and Kevin Heim for going above and beyond to ensure this tome was completed on a very tight schedule. Their hard work made the completion of this book a tremendously appreciated Christmas gift not only to this author, but also to every reader who may enjoy it (and I hope you are many!).

# TABLE OF CONTENTS

# PREFACE

Mike Nero (a.k.a., Beowolf) created by Christofer Nigro

Merry Christmas, Cool Yule, and Happy Holidays – the latter in case, yanno, you're an atheist and bitch about non-secular holiday greetings (just trying to be fair and polite to everyone!). This is Mike Nero, who is here to offer you season's greetings, to thank you for buying this book, to beg you not to return it for a refund (no shame here; it's not like you can buy food with dignity), and to curse you out and threaten to bite you if you happened to pirate it. The whole nine yards of thanking, begging, and cursing.

In case the pic below wasn't fucking obvious enough, I'm a werewolf. If you want to know more about me, you can read about my tragic early years as a vengeance-seeking teen lycanthrope in Wild Hunt Press's *Nero* series of novels; and about my adult self after I grew out of that angsty shit – well, kinda mostly did, anyway – and a became a monster hunter who protects humans, you need to get Wild Hunt Press's *Boogey Knights: Dark Warriors* anthology, along with checking out the upcoming series in *Mansion of the Macabre* and likely another series of novels.

But I'm not here just to promote myself (okay, maybe just a little) or plug other books by Wild Hunt Press… too much. I'm also here to boast and show off how these days I can morph into a full wolf form rather than my usual, more terrifying hybrid mode. And to further show off what I managed to steal, just for fun, from Christmas Village so I can boast about how fast and stealthy I am in this form. Just don't tell the Guy in Red, because he's only jolly and fun when you don't piss him off.

I'm also wondering if any of you happen to know how to get blood and sticky candy out of grayish fur. Then again, never mind, as I figure not too many folks outside of me ever experience that particular problem.

Okay, enough going on tangents not related to my real purpose for being here. Which is to tell you all about the tome you have in your hands. Or, happen to be reading on your tablet or phone. Whichever. In case the title and cover weren't clear enough, this book is about horror tales with a Christmas theme. The tradition of connecting horror and the festive season was once a popular thing when Santa's culturally distinct predecessors routinely hung out with demonic guys like the Krampus in the 18th century and ghost stories revolving around Yule were a popular thing to publish during the 19$^{th}$ century.

But publishers of horror comics kept this nasty tradition alive during the horror boom of the 1970s. And then we got certain perverse movies featuring serial killers dressing up as Santa during the '80s, a novel idea first introduced by Warren Publications and Marvel Comics in the '70s.

Since cool ideas that offend the sensitive should never go out of style, prose began picking up these traditions in the 2010s and '20s. Wild Hunt Press decided to give it a shot and enter the fray with its own depraved volume of horror-themed Christmas tales guaranteed to spoil your holiday cheer. The first publication from Wild Hunt in that ignoble genre is the volume you're now reading. This one is mostly the product of a single author, Christofer Nigro, the same dude who for some reason has the inclination to bring you my stories (don't ask me; I'm not qualified to give him a good psych evaluation).

Anywhos, in this tome you start off with "Santa Claws," where we explore the common fears experienced by kids stuck growing up in urban shitholes like Detroit. Eight-year-old Lyle Go's stubborn mom forces him to accompany her on foot to the store in the middle of the night to buy some sandwiches. Yes, you read that correctly: in the *middle of the night*. Just to get a few sandwiches! Of course, Lyle's dark imagination won't fail him, as there really are horrors out and about that chilly night on

Christmas Eve. And not only the typical type of predators that kids fear they and their moms may fall prey to, but also something decidedly *non-human* that is out to prove Lyle's mom isn't the only thing beset by late night hunger pangs. Needless to say, Lyle's final Christmas Eve in the world we know is not going to be a happy one.

Next up is "Jingle Hell," where Mr. N brings you a wickedly savage and utterly offensive take on a popular Christmas horror trope: the alpha serial killer who dresses up like Santa to commit waves of bloody mayhem during the holidays, proving that humans make some of the most horrific monsters one can imagine (or meet in real life). You've doubtless read or watched numerous horrid tales about brutal serial killers (and if you haven't, I wouldn't recommend reading this yarn!), but I'll wager my two front fangs that Virgil Kennedy is among the nastiest of the bunch. Don't say you weren't warned!

Then we get to "Silver and Mold," a yarn that taps into the older tradition of holiday horrors. The N guy (don't take that abbreviation the wrong way!) brings you a Christmas ghost story that seeks to terrify with its implications rather than mortify with gory imagery. This one provides a tear-jerker of a tragedy surrounding the type of real-world event that all of us dread the possibility of experiencing: the mysterious disappearance of a loved one that goes unsolved. Now imagine the unending torment that protagonist Linda Laughton deals with when her young BFF vanishes right under her nose on Christmas Eve when they were out and about together exploring a cemetery. (Why didn't they do this on Halloween? Just read and find out. Nigro has this covered!). The result is an unsettling mystery that literally comes back to haunt Linda and some of her new friends on the Christmas Eve marking the ten-year anniversary of the girl's disappearance.

Finally, Nigro brings you a special treat with "Yuletide Massacre Melee: The Convergence," which is nothing less than a tale that wraps up plot threads from each of the previous three tales yet can also be read as a standalone if you don't like reading shit in sequential order. It features a major surprise guest appearance by an entity you shouldn't really be surprised to find in a Christmas anthology. You'll see what I mean when you read the damn thing.

More finally still, you get a bonus guest yarn by Dustin Dreyling, the guy who authored the daijkaiju horror novel *Primordial Soup: The First Batch* and made many contributions to Wild Hunt Press anthology series, such as *Attack of the Kaiju*; *Duel of the Monsters*; and *Boogey Knights* – and like it or not, you're gonna see a lot more of this guy's stuff in the future. Since no Christmas horror anthology would be complete without the Krampus, you get a tale featuring the nasty horned holiday guy in Dreyling's short story "Nice Try." This volume's tale by the D-man is one that was given away as a free PDF gift to Wild Hunt Press's readers on the previous year's Christmas. You now get it in officially published form for the first time.

So, before I get into trouble should a wandering sentient reindeer or an animate snowman catch me with Santa's spare hat and the big ass candy cane he keeps for when he needs a sugar rush, I'm going to vacate Christmas Village by way of a portal found in the Mansion of the Macabre. Merry meet and merry part, and don't let the holidays kill you!

# SANTA CLAWS

Christmas was just three and a half hours away, but eight-year-old Lyle Goldberg was not in a happy or festive mood. No one of any age who was out walking the late-night streets of Detroit possibly could be. Yet, here he was, practically dragged across the dismal, dingy neighborhoods by his mother, Maude, who insisted on going out and buying a few sandwiches that she was having cravings for. Her financial situation as a single parent was such that she refused to take the car and waste any gas when the store she wanted to patronize was within a seven-block radius.

Of course, Maude could not care less about the fact that it was 20 degrees Fahrenheit with a whipping wind chill factor. Or, of the fact that the neighborhoods in this section of the declining city were not safe during the daylight hours, let alone this late at night. Visible signs of the holiday season, e.g., half-working Christmas lights decorating some homes and a few half-collapsed snowmen standing like statues on various lawns, were evident. Otherwise, the night was dead silent save for the occasional "whooshing" of the winds. The snow whirled about to create the appearance of an eerie, mist-permeated urban landscape where any possible bad thing Lyle's vivid imagination could possibly conceive had the possibility of happening.

The young boy would soon learn he was not wrong.

"Stop daydreaming and move your ass!" Maude shouted at her molasses-legged son. "I want to get to the store and pick up those sandwiches before it closes!"

"Mom, it's bad out here tonight," Lyle replied in a nervous tone. "I think we should go home and order some food."

"No one is delivering this late on Christmas Eve! Stop being so goddamned lazy that you can't go out for a little walk. Shit, you walk farther than this to get to school."

"But that's in the daytime, Mom."

He was about to ask his mother why she couldn't have just left him at home instead of forcing the boy to accompany her. But he decided not to, as he knew how her temper flared whenever he became defiant of her demands. And also, because in a strange way he was very worried that due to the dangers of the Detroit streets after dark she might not have come home had she ventured out alone. The boy dreaded how he would be sitting there watching the clock with his heart pounding like an internal piledriver every single second until she arrived home safely. He would sometimes have an anxiety attack if she was the least bit past the time she said the trip to the store would take.

Lyle's horrid imagination brought him to the point of panic over the thought of the police knocking on his door to tell him that his mom had been raped and murdered by some lunatic pervert. Instead, he hoped and prayed that if such individuals were out and about on this dreary Christmas Eve, they just might show mercy to a woman if she was accompanied by a child and overlook her in favor of some other target.

The boy thus decided to suck it up and get the late-night visit to the store over and done with quickly. He wrapped his winter coat tightly about himself while doing his best to fend off the cold and keep up the pace with his mother as they trudged through a quarter inch of snow.

All was almost tolerable until they passed an alley-like space between one tenement building and another. Lyle looked to his right and saw a figure silhouetted within a blowing wall of snow standing within that passageway. The boy squinted his eyes to make out the figure in more detail and saw that it was... well, Santa Claus.

Christofer Nigro
*Santa Claws*
Yuletide Horrors Volume 1


The man in red looked exactly like popular imagery had conditioned Lyle to see him: a tall but corpulent gentleman in a full body suit of scarlet, black buckled belt with matching ebony gloves & boots, white cotton-like frills around the sleeves, and rosy cheeks on a head with a long billowy white beard and a red hat that matched his outfit. The Santa figure smiled and waved to the boy as soon as the latter saw him.

Lyle found himself more alarmed than excited, however, as there seemed to be something "off" about this Santa. The biggest such reason was that the old fellow's smile looked more like a vile grin than an affable beam. Further, the beaming man's teeth seemed yellow and crooked in a way he would have found difficult to put into words.

"Mom, look!" Lyle shouted almost reflexively. "Between those buildings! It's Santa!"

Maude responded by grabbing her lagging son by his right arm and roughly pulling him forward to keep pace with her.

"Will you just come on!"

"But didn't you see him, Mom? It was Santa!"

"I looked, but it was just Mrs. Morris. You know, the nice old lady who always gives us cookies and cake? She lives in the building right next to that alley."

"Mom, it wasn't her! It was honestly Santa!"

"It was Mrs. Morris! She's fat and the blowing snow may have made her look like Santa to you. Now, come on and let's go! Or Santa will bring you nothing this year!"

At this point, the only thing the thoroughly freaked out little boy wanted from Santa was for him and his mom to be transported safely off those streets. But if who he saw in the alley *was* actually Santa Claus – and the boy *knew* that it was *not* sweet Mrs. Morris – then he wanted absolutely nothing from Santa, now or forevermore.

Maude then grabbed her son's wrist and pulled him across the street as she picked up the stride to reach their point of destination. Lyle now had the feeling that his mom also sensed that they should get off these late-night streets as quickly as possible, and that something truly awful was out and about this Christmas Eve. However, much as the boy feared, his mother remained too stubborn to call off their quest and return home now that they were halfway to the store.

Crossing that street was easy, as there appeared to be no cars out and about that evening. Just Lyle and his mom… and, evidently, someone else who may have been either Santa Claus or nice Mrs. Morris, depending on whether you asked mother or son.

Little were the two aware that they were being followed at the end of the street by a notorious local drunkard by the name of Phil Edwards. This unkempt man was a well-known but rather unwelcome presence in the local neighborhoods. Sporting a dilapidated coat that barely did the job of keeping him warm in cold weather, he was easily identifiable with his beige Hooligan hat.

Phil had always had a "thing" for Maude Goldberg, as he referred to it when he discussed it with fellow hobos, and he believed that this quiet winter night with no one else around would be the perfect time for him to corner the woman and ask her out. The presence of her little boy would be no deterrent to the persistent man.

When the mother and son were almost at the end of the block, Phil picked up speed to catch up with them. As he passed in front of the alley, however, he turned around when he clearly heard a gruff but pleasantly familiar voice call his name from within the space between buildings. Phil turned to see the figure of a man whose features were somewhat obscured by the wind blowing clouds of snow through the alley.

"Who's there?" he asked before taking another swig from the bottle of Ripple in his hand.

The figure moved closer and revealed himself to be none other than Richard Greenwald, the social worker who had been one of the very few people to show genuine concern for Phil as he struggled with his problems over the past two years.

"Rich, is that you, man?" Phil enquired.

"Yes, it's me, my friend," Rich confirmed with a smile. "Have you been drinking again? And following that woman again? After our last discussion?"

Phil never asked or seemed to be concerned about the most obvious question, however: What was Rich doing there at that time of night and in that kind of weather, far from where his own home was located? No, for some reason, all that mattered to Phil was that this valued presence in his life was there and would help him avoid doing something stupid that might get him tossed into the slammer again.

Phil stepped into the alley and approached Rich as he admitted, "Yeah, I guess I had a bit too much again tonight, man. But since you're here, can we talk?"

Rich's only response was to raise his arms and make a growling sound at Phil. The counselor then opened his mouth ravenously as he effortlessly pulled the drunkard into the alley. The side of each tenement wall that formed the lane were spattered with Phil's blood as the individual he believed to be Richard Greenwald tore him to shreds. The hobo only managed to let off a brief scream of terror that Lyle and Maude were by that time too far away to hear.

***

As the two evening trekkers walked towards a nearby building on the other side of the street, they suddenly heard a familiar melodious clanging sound. When they passed the source, mother and son turned to see that it was a man in a Santa Claus suit jingling a large bell and sitting in front of a metal donation coffer with "Salvation Army" painted on it. Lyle was rattled a second time in under ten minutes by the sight of a Santa that gave him an extremely bad feeling, even though this one was obviously a different man than the previous figure he saw.

The second Santa turned to see Maude and Lyle walking by him from about twenty feet away and gave them a wide beam. "Care to come over here and donate a few coins to needy kids, ma'am?"

"No, I'm sorry," Maude hastily responded. "I'm a bit low on cash tonight."

"Cunt!" the apparent Salvation Army employee said loud enough for both mother and son to hear as his frown morphed into an angry scowl.

Maude resisted the urge to utter a rebuttal, feeling it was best to again grab her son by the wrist and pull him with her as she quickly picked up her pace. She knew that the sandwich shop, which stayed open past 10 PM even on Christmas Eve, was just at the end of the next block. The woman wanted to make haste in reaching it rather than confronting that man in the Santa suit and made a mental note to take a route home that avoided this corner.

"I'm gonna call the Salvation Army and report that asshole tonight," she said aloud in front of her son in order to vent. "They seriously need to be careful of who they hire to collect donations during the Christmas season."

Lyle could see that his mom was increasingly coming to his line of thinking about going out at this time of night just to fetch some sandwiches. However, he also knew that she would never admit that to him, especially not when they were so close to their destination. The boy was still hoping that his mother would ask Jimmy, the proprietor of the sandwich shop, if they could remain there until he closed at around 11 PM and drive them home.

The two were abruptly taken aback while approaching the middle of the block to find themselves face-to-face with a tall, lanky older man who appeared to be of Indian descent. This gentleman had light brown skin and salt & pepper colored hair with a well-trimmed beard of the same hue. His eyes were a piercing gray and he looked down intensely at the two younger people who had almost walked into him. He was standing in front of the Hindi curio shop called *Sasta Maal* and would have been recognized by Maude Goldberg had she ever stepped in there before.

Maude let out a brief startled scream. Her son did the same in tandem.

"Oh, I'm so sorry," Maude practically stammered. Hazy wisps of freezing carbon dioxide left her mouth in profuse little clouds as she struggled to catch her breath. "I-I'm so sorry, sir. We didn't see you there—"

"That is okay," the man replied in a soft foreign accent. "I failed to see you in the blowing snow also. My name is Karam. I own this shop here."

"I'm—I'm Maude, and it looks like a nice shop. But I've got to go, I'm in a hurry."

Even though that was the truth, Maude, like her startled son, could not get away from the strange Indian man's presence fast enough. They quickly crossed the street and headed down to the shop called Jimmy's Superior Sandwiches.

As they were now a mere sixty feet from their point of destination, Lyle turned to notice that the first Santa he had seen in the alley was now walking behind them several yards down the block. He moved at a rapid but steady pace. The chill that Lyle was already feeling from the cold intensified with a sudden surge of fear, as he could not understand how this Santa Claus could possibly be there unless he was deliberately following them.

"Mom, Santa's here again," the boy said as he raced to keep in stride with his mother. "He's right behind us."

"Enough!" Maude shouted back. "The store is right there, so just hurry up!"

The woman again dragged her son along at a greater pace seconds before they both reached the door of the sandwich shop and stepped in.

As Karam Dhavale watched the mother and son enter Jimmy's Superior Sandwich's from across the street, he likewise noticed the figure following them as it entered his field of view. Only what he saw was not anything resembling the popular phenotype of Santa Claus. Due to a lifetime of spiritual training connected to the Hindu religion in his native India, Karam could clearly see the true form of what was behind them.

The entity tracking the mother and son could be seen through Karam's unhindered vision as a bulky man-shaped beast just over seven feet in height with dark brown skin that appeared to be without clothing; a long mane of wild bushy hair; a monstrous face resembling a Hindu ritual mask; two long tusk-like teeth protruding from the upper part of its wide mouth and thick lips, and claw-like talons extending from its enormous hands.

*"Kyaa!"* Karam exclaimed to himself. "That is a *rakshasa*. Those two are being hunted by the shape-shifting demon, one of Brahma's darkest creations."

People who were familiar with Vedic theology, like Karam, were well aware of the legends of the *Rakshasa* – legendary demonic beings with an insatiable lust for the flesh and blood of mortal and god alike. They were said to be inadvertently created by the exhalations of the sleeping creator-deity Brahma. This species relentlessly hunted humans as prey and were greatly aided in this ghastly pursuit by advanced glamour skills that enabled them to lure and disorient their prey by disguising themselves as the person their target trusted the most – this image being pulled telepathically from the victim's mind.

These demons were allegedly banished to another realm of existence thousands of years ago by the Hindu gods. Legend had it that they could periodically return to Earth in small numbers to seek out victims on this plane of reality again to determine if human civilization reached a point where the evil, corrupt side of the mortal species had become ascendant – at which time the bestial *rakshasa* could be sent over *en masse* to take this globe by force. Reports of increased rakshasa attacks during the tumultuous 20th century were making their way throughout the American Hindu communities and included a notable one alleging to have taken place a year or two earlier in the Roosevelt Heights section of Chicago.

Karam considered rushing back into his shop to see if he could find a weapon among its Hindu novelty items to use against this beast and protect the woman and child it was stalking. However, he came to conclude that while he was no coward and would take measures to protect his own life and store from this threat, he was likewise no hero. Taking on a rakshasa for people he did not know and who obviously did not care to get to know him was a risk he determined was not worth taking.

Accordingly, the spiritual man stepped into the safety of his shop and silently wished the mother and son luck in surviving this Christmas Eve.

\*\*\*

As Maude and Lyle entered the sandwich shop, less than a half hour before closing time, they both immediately noticed that Jimmy was not behind the counter as was usually the case. Instead, a younger white man in a pair of oversized bifocals who appeared to be in his 30s with unkempt, longish dark blonde hair was tending the cash register. Maude almost felt as if this man resembled a hideous cast-out from a Hippie commune, and Lyle likewise recoiled from the "vibes" this man in a dirty Pink Floyd shirt gave off. The whole atmosphere of the shop seemed to have a disquieting pall over it because of being under the watch of this odd individual.

"Um… hi," Maude greeted the man nervously.

"Hello there!" the man replied with great enthusiasm and a cringe-inducing grin.

"Is… Jimmy here tonight?" Maude asked.

"No, he's not. He got invited to something or other by his family for Christmas Eve. I'm Sammy, and he hired me to run the place tonight."

"Oh. I'm… Maude. And this is my son, Lyle."

Sammy reached his hand out to the two, apparently for shaking purposes. Maude did so with just a few of his fingers before quickly pulling away.

The man frowned but quickly forced a smile back upon his homely face. "It will be a pleasure to help a nice and beautiful woman like you, Maude. What can I make for you here?"

Usually, Maude would have Jimmy make her a sandwich by hand from the fresh meat stored behind the counter. This time, however, she elicited a quiet sigh of relief from Lyle by opting for another, atypical option.

"Um, I'm in a hurry and I know you're closing in just a few minutes," Maude rejoined, "so I'm just going to grab one of the ready-made sandwiches from the fridge in the back."

"Oh, no, it would be no bother at all," Sammy countered with another disquieting grin. "I wouldn't mind staying open a bit longer than I have to for you to get a freshly made sandwich. In fact, it would be my pleasure to do that for you. Not too many sexy women come in here, ya know. So, what type of sandwich could I make for you?"

Maude pulled her son towards the back of the shop by his sleeve, towards one of the glass-covered refrigeration units located there. "I told you, Sammy, it's okay. I'm in a rush so I'm just gonna grab two pre-wrapped turkey sandwiches from the back."

"Suit yourself," Sammy said in a grumbling tone as he tossed down the knife he was about to use to make her a sandwich. "But I told you it wouldn't be any bother."

"Mom, let's get out of here," Lyle whispered to Maude as they reached the refrigeration units in the back of the shop. "Please? I don't like it here."

"We are, okay?" she replied nervously. "Just shut up and grab two turkey sandwiches. I'm trying to get a few dollars ready here so I can just place it on the counter, and he can cash us out as quickly as possible."

As Lyle carefully selected two of the correct sandwiches while his mom counted the dollars she had in her purse, the former briefly turned to look towards the door they were determined to head out of as fast as possible. There he saw the figure of Santa Claus standing just outside as if waiting for someone to leave... and the boy had no doubt whom that was.

"Mom!" he said in a voice of near-panic. "Santa is standing outside the door!"

"Shut the fuck up!" was all the now frantic woman said as she grabbed the sandwiches from his hands and hurried up to the counter.

Upon reaching it, Maude dropped several dollars near the cash register. Sammy snatched up the greenbacks and quickly counted them before opening the register.

"Thanks, beautiful lady," he said in his low nasally voice. "Let me get you your change."

"No, it's okay!" she said in an anxious tone as she took the sandwiches and headed for the door. "You can keep it."

"Okay, thanks, but listen!" Sammy stated as he moved from behind the counter and walked towards her and Lyle. "I'm closing right now, and it's dark and cold out there, so I'll give you and your son a ride home. It would be no bother. I like you."

"No!" she rejoined louder than she intended. "Thank you, but no. We live close, we don't mind walking. Have a Merry Christmas."

"But I told you, it would be no bother!" Sammy countered insistently.

"No, thank you, I said," was Maude's equally insistent reply as she pulled her son by his coat's upper sleeve towards the door.

"Wait," Sammy implored again. "Don't you want a bag for those sandwiches?"

"No, we're fine!" Maude decreed as she pushed the door open and pulled her son out with her.

It was empty and unnervingly quiet outside in the darkened streets, and there was no sign of Santa Claus, whom Lyle believed he had seen just outside the door about thirty seconds earlier. Despite a sense of momentary relief, the boy shuddered as he realized they now had to walk the same distance back through these streets in order to get home. Should they have taken the offer of a ride from Sammy, he wondered? The conclusion that immediately came back to him was that they were damned if they did and damned if they didn't.

"Mom, can we hurry home?" Lyle queried anxiously. *"Please?"*

"Yes, let's hurry up! But watch that you don't slip on the ice!"

Maude had no argument with her son's frenetic insistence on getting home fast – especially since she knew Sammy would be closing the shop and leaving in under a minute. And she strongly suspected the unsettling man would do so with haste, so he that had a chance of catching her before she and her son had walked off the block.

The fears of mother and son alike turned out to have been correct, as less than twenty seconds later, Sammy stepped out of the shop and secured its double lock for the evening. The skeevy man turned and grinned with satisfaction as he noticed that Maude and Lyle had not yet turned to the next block and hence were still within his view. He realized that he could catch up to them and persuade the woman to let him drive her and the boy back to their home... and that maybe Maude would even be grateful enough to let him talk her into inviting him in for some hot cocoa.

As Sammy took his car keys from his pocket, however, he suddenly heard the voice of an older woman call his name from behind. It was a familiar one from his past, and he turned to see none other than the smiling figure of Mrs. Caldwell, the only teacher in the orphanage where he grew up that treated him with kindness. Sammy never did know what happened to her after he was "let go" from the place upon turning eighteen so many years ago, but he still could not help being comforted by the sight.

"Sammy?" she said in her pleasant melodious voice. "You shouldn't be spending Christmas Eve alone. I always tried making it special for you and the other kids back at Finster Hall, and I can still do that for you now."

"Mrs. Caldwell," Sammy stated quietly, dropping his keys as he smiled to once again see virtually the only person to ever treat him compassionately. He began walking towards her with open arms. "You always made me feel special. You looked me up and tracked me here just to spend Christmas Eve with me?"

"I certainly did! And what a fine and handsome man you have become. I will be so happy to have you for over for dinner, my dear boy."

As Sammy moved closer to her, Mrs. Caldwell suddenly leapt through the air at him like a pouncing cat, her mouth open wide and salivating. The beast landed on top of Sammy with crushing force as it began slicing off his clothing and flesh with its eagle-like talons and tearing into him with its tusk-like teeth. The man screamed in horror and agony, but within several seconds little was left but a skeleton laying in a spot of sidewalk surrounded by scarlet-stained snow, bits of stray flesh & internal organs, and shreds of bloody & tattered clothing.

Maude and Lyle had just crossed the street to where the *Sasta Maal* was located when they heard Sammy's screams and the sound of skin and clothing being ripped to shreds. They turned to see a hulking dark form partly concealed by a snow drift as it swiftly and ravenously stripped the man's skeleton of its flesh and organs and devoured them with the zeal of a starving dog.

They both screamed, thus alerting the beast to their presence and reminding the vile creature that its original targets were still in the vicinity. The figure leapt from the sidewalk into the middle of the street in a single bound like a king-size monkey. It then began running across the street towards them in a diagonal direction.

Maude dropped the sandwiches she carried and pushed her son violently forward.

"Lyle, run! Run towards home!"

The mother and son raced the several blocks towards their cheap apartment located at a nearby complex, all the way struggling to run over snow, avoid slipping on ice, and still retain their sense of direction despite the clouds of misty snow that blew in their faces. Their adrenaline had sufficiently fueled their flight response to get them to navigate most of the way before experiencing a debilitating degree of fatigue.

They neither saw nor heard any sign of the figure pursuing them, but they were admittedly only paying attention to where they were going. As the two reached the front door of their apartment, Maude scrambled to the get the keys from her pocket.

"Mom, hurry!"

"Shut up! You're making me fucking nervous, and I can't find the keys!"

"Hello, Lyle," came the cheerful voice of an older man from behind him.

The boy turned to see Santa Claus standing on the sidewalk leading up to their front door.

"Can I come in for some cookies and milk?" the jolly, red-suited figure with the disturbing grin asked politely.

"Mom!" the boy screeched in horror. "It's Santa! I-I think he's the monster!"

Maude turned and looked at the figure her son's terrified scream mentioned. To her son's surprise, she let out a huge sigh of relief upon doing so.

"Hi, Ms. Goldberg," came the cheery voice of Mrs. Morris. "Are you having trouble with your key? Those locks are really a pain when they freeze up during the winter."

"Yes," Maude replied. "But… it's not safe out here, Mrs. Morris. There's, um, some type of dangerous killer animal out here! We saw it kill someone! Please, come inside with us so none of us have to be alone tonight."

"You are such a dear," Mrs. Morris said as she walked towards the door in acceptance of the offer.

"Mom!" Lyle screamed. "That's not Mrs. Morris! It's Santa! Don't you see? I think he's the monster! I think it can make itself look differently to different people! Don't let him in!"

"Shut up and get in here, Lyle!" Maude hollered as she stepped in the house right behind the cheerfully smiling Mrs. Morris.

"Mom! Nooooooo…!"

Lyle backed away from the front door of what should have been the sanctuary of his home. It was then that he heard his mom scream in terror alongside the sound of a snarling beast. Maude went quiet with jarring suddenness as the screams and growls were replaced by the loud smacking and slurping noises of an animal voraciously feeding alongside the distinct sound of clothing being torn up. A growing pool of blood filled with pieces of something that resembled uncooked meat from the butcher's market spilled out onto the welcome mat just outside the front door.

The boy, now in shock, backed away further as Santa ran outside with a wider smile than ever before, of the type Lyle imagined the jolly old man would have after finishing a nice serving of milk and cookies. Except that his mouth and white beard were covered with blood that the boy realized had once been flowing in his mother's veins. Santa retained that devilish smile as he bared his crooked, blood-and-flesh caked teeth and reached his arms out towards the boy.

"Now, do not fret over missing out on the first dinner of the night, Lyle," the beast posing as Santa stated while licking his chops. "Because you now get to be guest of honor at my second one!"

Lyle Goldberg forced his legs to move as he ran out into the cold, bitter streets of Detroit with a monstrosity he perceived in the image of Santa Claus in hot pursuit. The boy's final Christmas Eve on these streets would certainly turn out to be eventful, to say the least.

# END

# JINGLE HELL

Virgil Kennedy was to receive the greatest Christmas present an institutionalized serial killer like himself could ever hope for: a pair of the laziest security guards he had ever met were hired by the mental hospital where he resided just a few days before Christmas Eve circa 1977.

As the special night arrived, the guards were too busy watching the Movie of the Week on the office television the same evening that cable had finally been installed as a present for all patients and employees. In case anyone reading this happens to care, the distracting movie in question just happened to be *Steel Avenger,* a live action TV movie re-enacting the life of the eccentric and adventurous industrialist Howard Hughes and his ill-fated attempts to play public hero in a suit of powered exo-armor.

It turned out that Virgil actually did care since he found the movie entertaining, and he watched a fourth of it alongside the two inept guards while wearing the uniform of an orderly he had secretly killed and afterwards hid the body in a broom closet. The two newbie security officers were so involved with the film and amusing each other with amusing anecdotes they each heard about the recently deceased Hughes that they never noticed that the "orderly" visiting their office was actually one of the patients.

Virgil quickly dispatched the would-be guards by dissolving an overdose of crushed sedatives into the coffee he brewed and served for them. He had been more than patient enough to display good and even nurturing behavior towards his fellow violent detainees over the past few years in order to gain increasing amounts of trust and decreasing levels of security. In fact, he had become a respected fake model patient whose goal, as he often told his doctors, was indeed to return to good society one day – but only so he could go on another brutal murder spree, which he had neglected to mention during his sessions.

Having fooled them all, Virgil's first three kills in six years made him ecstatic as he quietly sat between the two dead men watching the closing credits of *Steel Avenger*. Though Virgil had been thrilled to kill again, doing so in such a subtle fashion, the way so many of his female counterparts tended to operate, made him feel like a sissy.

"Too easy, Virgil," he said to himself while shaking his head as the two unsuspecting guards took their first sips of the tainted java.

"Huh?" one of them said as he overheard the remark.

"You'll find out in just a few seconds, man," Virgil quietly responded. "In the meantime, this movie is pretty far out, so if I were you, I'd watch as much of it as you can before you croak off."

"Say what?" the other guard exclaimed as he studied the orderly sitting between and just behind him and his partner for the first time since the man had entered the room an hour ago.

"I think you heard me," Virgil replied. "Now, if you don't mind, I think the movie is getting to the part where Hughes gets trashed and tries to fuck a woman with the armor on."

"Wait a minute," the second guard said. "You ain't no orderly. Aren't you…?"

Virgil calmly nodded. "Yup. I sure am, you stupid shit."

"Donny!" the second guard shouted as he reached for his billy club. "This guy is…"

No sooner did the security man unsheathe his nightstick than it fell out of his hand and clattered on the floor while his eyes rolled into his head. Virgil had made sure that he didn't skimp on the dosage of sedative he dissolved in that decanter of coffee.

The first guard, Donny, managed to lift his club over his head and scream, "You son of a bitch!" before he too suddenly went limp and sank down into his chair into a sleep which he would never awaken from.

"Save your harsh words for yourself, idjit," Virgil muttered as Donny uttered a soft, hissing death rattle.

"Always music to my ears," was the triumphant killer's response to the final sound uttered by the guard. "Thank you for being such fools and getting hired anyway, gents. Oh, and Merry Christmas! You certainly made my list!"

After quietly watching the rest of the movie, Virgil took the uniform and keys from one of the dead cops that would grant him egress from the minimum-security wing of the mental hospital. Realizing it was a very cold evening in the heart of Detroit's worst section of neighborhoods, he made sure to take a heavy coat with him. He also absconded with one of the guards' billy clubs and a kitchen knife he had stolen from the cafeteria.

Virgil smiled with the glee of a child eagerly awaiting the many gifts coming to him on Christmas morning when the cold winter air touched his face upon exiting the back of the facility. This section of Detroit had numerous abandoned buildings and dark alleyways he could hide in as well as find numerous targets to satiate his unquenchable lust for killing. It was roughly 10 PM, perfect for him to scout the dismal urban environs that he once again called home.

His bright blue eyes scanned the rows of dilapidated tenements – some inhabited by low-rent residents, others empty save for non-paying squatters and heroin addicts enjoying their fix – and he was confronted by a three-dimensional panorama of urban decay and a system gone wrong.

"Man, I love Detroit," he whispered aloud to himself as he hopped a fence that separated the back of the facility from the outside environment.

Virgil began exploring in earnest, seeing few people around. It was a cold night in a bleak area of the city with only intermittent examples of semi-working lights adorning the various decrepit buildings to indicate the holiday season. After all, how many people here were truly happy and filled with hope, whether on this or any other night? Virgil certainly didn't count himself among these despondent masses. As a certified psychopath, he was effectively unable to experience such a range of emotions, and merely gained *satisfaction* along with a surge of orgasmic ecstasy by doing what he did best.

That was more than enough for Virgil, however. Not being able to kill for six years, save for the "quickie" murder of the orderly and the "sissy" way he whacked the two security guards during the past few hours, left him yearning to get back to the work that was so rudely interrupted when some fool detective managed to arrest him half a decade ago.

As Virgil approached one corner intersection, he was drawn to an incessant tinkling sound emanating from down the street. He turned to see an elderly employee of the Salvation Army dressed like Santa Claus and jingling a bell in front of a metal donation coffer.

"Good evening and Merry Christmas," the affable old gentlemen greeted Virgil with a smile. "Would you care to donate a few coins to help local needy kids this holiday season?"

Virgil smiled widely as he walked closer to Santa's dedicated helper. "Why, of course, good sir. I most certainly have something here for you."

"Oh, wonderful, wonderful!" the excited gent said in imitation of his idol, Lawrence Welk. "You are quite smartly dressed this evening, sir. Are you a security guard?"

"Nah, I just stole the suit from one that I killed," Virgil said casually as he smacked the old man over the skull with his billy club.

The gent twitched and gagged as blood gushed out of a tear atop his bald head. Virgil then quickly placed his baton around the injured man's throat and dragged him into the thin alley beside the Salvation Army center. It was dark and quiet in that part of the neighborhood, and Virgil wanted to take a bit of time bringing this old coot's life to an undeserved end.

The killer put his booted foot on the old man's throat, which choked him and forced his mouth open. Virgil then reached into his pocket and removed a pair of pliers he purloined from the hospital.

"Yeah, I'm most definitely in the Christmas spirit tonight, old man," he said to his hacking and bleeding victim. "Want to see how *much* in spirit I am?

"'All I want for Christmas is your two front teeth...'" Virgil paraphrased the popular holiday song as he used the pliers to rip out the old man's two upper incisors.

Christofer Nigro
*Jingle Hell*
Yuletide Horrors Volume 1

The man twitched and gasped in pain harder than before as blood poured out of the twin gaping wounds where his two front teeth had been.

"I'm impressed, man," Virgil said with a sadistic smile. "I expected them to be dentures! But they were the genuine article. Congrats on keeping your real pearly whites until the very end.

"And speaking of the end…"

Virgil swiftly shoved his baton into the old man's mouth, closing off the airways in his throat. He then placed his booted foot on the hardwood bludgeon and forced the nightstick upwards, crushing the rest of the old man's upper teeth and ripping the lower jawbone away from its connective tissue – all in a single quick movement.

The killer watched the old guy's spasming and gagging body for the next several seconds before raising the club and bringing it down on the man's forehead three times: once for fatality; twice for insurance; and thrice just for fun and venting his years of inactivity.

With the front of the old man's brow pulverized into fragments of bone and gray matter, Virgil dragged the corpse behind a large dumpster in the alley. He then stripped both himself and the dead old man, replacing his security guard uniform with the traditional raiment of Santa Claus worn by his victim.

"Nice how people I kill tend to have outfits that fit me," Virgil said quietly aloud as he tossed the nude body of the elderly guy inside the dumpster. "Thank you for the Christmas gift, old timer. It's a shame I can't be here to see the look on the face of the unfortunate soul who happens to come across *your* wrinkly naked and mutilated ass while taking out the trash. And it's a shame that it's too cold for your carcass to rot a little bit first. Ah well, the rats will probably take some flesh off of you, so you'll still look nice and horrible for whoever finds you."

As the new and dark helper of Santa turned to head towards the donation coffer, he gave the dumpster one final look. "Oh, and since I didn't say it before after you were nice enough to say it to me… Merry Christmas, old man. Hah. Hah."

*Now, let's see who wearing Santa's threads gives me easy access to tonight.*

## Christofer Nigro
### Jingle Hell
Yuletide Horrors Volume 1

The Santa-clad Virgil sat in front of the donation casket marked "Salvation Army" and attempted to look benign and sweet as he beamed a wide smile and began jingling the bell.

Within a few minutes a young woman accompanied by a little boy walked past the corner of Virgil's spot about twenty feet distant. The killer smiled when he saw them.

*Well, well, look what just walked into the spider's web. Who the hell was it who said that Christmas wasn't for killers? Heh!*

Virgil put on his widest fake smile and spoke to the woman as she walked by. "Care to come over here and donate a few coins to needy kids, ma'am?"

When they turned around, Virgil was surprised to see the look of alarm on the boy's face at the sight of a Salvation Army Santa. *Is that kid a fucking psychic or something?*

"No, I'm sorry," the woman hastily responded. "I'm a bit low on cash tonight."

"Cunt!" was Virgil's only response, his profound disappointment causing him to say it loud enough for the mother and son at the corner to hear him.

As the two picked up speed and crossed the street to the right of him to vanish from his sight, the killer considered going after them as quietly as possible.

*Nah,* he decided to himself. *I somehow spooked them enough to get a few kicks out of it. Let someone else disguised as Santa follow their asses tonight. I think I would look way too conspicuous wandering around the streets like this anyway. Someone else is bound to come along sooner or later this fine Christmas Eve...*

"Hey, mac, are you okay?"

The Virgil-cum-Santa looked up to see that the surly voice came from a uniformed officer out on a solo beat. *Oh shit. Gotta hold it together, Virg! The "Man" has arrived.*

"Why, hello, Officer," Virgil said in his best faux kindly voice. "And Merry Christmas to you. Would you like to donate a few coins to the needy kids of Detroit tonight?"

"I actually came to ask if you were okay and if you had happened to see anything unusual on the streets tonight. How long have you been out here?"

"Oh, I've been jingling the bell for a few hours now, sir. What kind of unusual things are you talking about anyway? This is Detroit. There's always something unusual going on. I hope it isn't more racial issues. Not on Christmas Eve. This time of the year is supposed to be about peace."

"I don't want to alarm you, fella. But there has been a slew of… violent deaths around the Brush Park area tonight. I was told that the Salvation Army would have a Santa on duty outside their building tonight, so I decided to come down and see that you get home safely. You aren't gonna get anyone out sparing change anymore tonight. You did your part for hours now, so let me give you a ride home."

*Hmmm, I would have really loved to have had that lady and her kid to work my skills on, but this new opportunity that just fell into my lap is interesting enough. Merry Christmas again, Virgil!*

"As much as I hate to leave this post that I'm so dedicated to before midnight, I'm sure you know best, Officer. And I would never argue with an upstanding man of the law. I would be grateful if you gave me a ride home."

"Alright, my squad car is at the end of the street. Put your donation things in the office, lock it up for the night, and meet me there."

"Of course, sir."

As the cop walked over to the car with his vision partly obscured by the blowing snow drifts, Virgil simply pushed the donation coffer into the alleyway and pocketed the small amount of change inside, figuring it could always come in handy if he wanted to find a phone booth (one that really worked, that is) and make a threatening or obscene call to alarm some random fool he found in the White Pages. He then sauntered over to the police car at the corner, pretending to have a limp to further get under the officer's guard.

*I wonder what the fuzz meant by other killings in this area of the city tonight. I only made one kill so far after getting out of the hospital. Do I have some competition? Nah. It's probably just street gangs and drug dealers; the usual shit in this fun city.*

After pretending to hobble over to the squad car, Virgil gave Burns the following request: "Officer, would you mind if I sat in the front seat? Having been stuck in a P.O.W. camp for a few weeks during my tour in 'Nam, I get panic attacks when I'm behind anything that reminds me of a cage."

"Certainly," the officer graciously replied. "It's not like you're a criminal."

"Thank you so much, sir," the Killer Santa cheerfully responded.

"Ah, I see you're a vet," the policeman said as he prepared to put his key in the ignition. "Bless you for your service. Even if I can't imagine such a nice guy who enjoys playing Santa out in the cold to collect change for needy kids to have ever been capable of killing other people."

"Well, appearances can be quite deceiving, sir."

Virgil's astute adage was the last thing Officer Jack Burns heard before his jaw was broken when the Killer Santa suddenly whacked the officer with his pilfered nightstick. The killer then grabbed the lawman's head and banged it several times against the steering wheel, adding a fractured skill and a deviated septum to Burns' growing list of injuries.

Before the besieged cop could begin to recover his senses, he received a blow to the top of his skull by Virgil's billy club, which split his cranium in two. With part of his brain exposed, the soft gray tissues were mercilessly spattered all over the front seat by yet another salvo from Virgil's baton.

Burns' years on the force in Detroit made him a tough cop, so rather than losing consciousness, his reaction to the brutal assault was for him to vomit on the steering wheel and swing his arms around violently. He attempted to scream out a series of words that only came out as rambling moans and coughs.

"Feisty little bastard, aren't you, Officer?" the Killer Santa asked rhetorically as he brandished his filched kitchen knife. "That's okay, I don't mind working for my kills now and then."

Burns was no longer able to see or think clearly, so the back of his neck was easy pickings for a vicious slash by Virgil's blade. Blood seeped out of the deep wound like crimson syrup oozing from ruptured tree bark. As his strength began rapidly seeping out along with his life fluid, the serial killer wrapped a thin but powerful arm around the lawman's neck and pulled him halfway over the back seat. He then thrust the knife deep into the cop's left eye and twisted it savagely.

Within seconds, the oft-decorated Officer Jack Burns ceased struggling after releasing a final sound that resembled a cross between a moan and a gurgle.

"Okay," Virgil said to himself aloud, "with that done, it's time for Santa to go cruising the mean streets looking for lots of people to put on his naughty list. And this Christmas that list is gonna be longer than John Holmes' dick! Hah! Hah!"

The Santa-tressed killer quickly disembarked from the back of the squad car and opened the driver's door, pushing the heavy-set cadaver of Officer Burns onto the passenger side with surprising ease.

"Sorry, but you gotta make way for Santa, Officer."

Virgil then turned the key in the ignition and started the engine. The DPD squad car, now under the control of one of the nation's most notorious serial killers since Chainsaw Bubba and Rosscoe Everrest, took off into the snow-covered streets of Detroit.

"Santa Claus is comin' to town!" he began singing.

Within moments the car seemingly driven by Santa with a dead and bleeding cop sitting beside him turned a corner as Virgil spotted a hobo slumbering atop an underground vent to keep warm.

"He sees you when you're sleeping..." Virgil continued vocalizing as he ran over the snoozing vagrant and crushed him beneath the tires.

The killer then screeched the car to a halt in front of three African American youths, apparently siblings – a male and female teen and a boy of about twelve. The first of these looked quite athletic and was just over six feet in height; the girl was an average height of '5'4," and the twelve-year-old was quite tall for that age, standing about '5'7," despite the youth's "baby face" making his actual age evident. The trio were quite startled to see a car driven by Santa Claus with an open window in the freezing cold.

"He knows when you're awake!" Virgil resumed singing as he pointed Burns' 357 Magnum at the trio and fired off a shot.

The high caliber projectile flew into the open mouth of the stunned teen girl and blew the back of her head completely off.

The older teen boy and his younger male sibling screamed in horror as their sister's brains spattered all over them, the streetlight beside them, and the snow-covered sidewalk around them. The terror-stricken duo came to their senses and ran towards a nearby brick apartment complex with a level of speed indicating good athletic capacity. Virgil took another shot, this one blowing a fist-sized hole in the younger boy's right calf. The youth screamed in agony, but his older brother was quick enough to catch the boy in his arms before he could fall on the slushy ground.

"Merry Christmas, motherfuckers!" Virgil laughed as he pointed the revolver in preparation for taking a third shot.

"We gotta get the fuck out of here!" the older boy yelled as he lifted his seriously injured younger brother and carried him behind a dumpster.

Virgil fired two more shots, but all he heard was the sound of projectiles denting the metal of the huge blue metallic refuse container. Then the chamber went empty.

*"Pardonne-moi,* Officer," Virgil said to Burns' stiffening corpse as he dropped the empty revolver and opened the driver's door. "But Santa needs to deal with the latest on his naughty list up close and personal."

The older teen sequestered behind the dumpster had removed his scarf and tied it tightly around the younger boy's leg just above the large bullet wound. He prayed it would staunch the bleeding and give his little brother the chance to survive that his sister had just lost.

"Aaagghh… Jake, it hurts," the boy said in an agonized tone. "And… and Cecilia is… dead."

"I know, Lem," Jake said in a low and somber voice. "I did what I could to stop the bleeding. Now try to get to help while I hold that fucker off."

"Jake, don't leave me…"

"You have to leave me here now, Lem! Go! I don't know if I can stop this fucking maniac. It's your only chance!"

The deeply sobbing Lemuel Oliver used a crutch his brother had just found in the dumpster to stagger off to safety, doing his best to keep his injured leg elevated. Jake rifled around in the large garbage bin hoping to find anything that could be used as a weapon as his badly injured little brother disappeared down the street towards an unknown fate.

At last Jake came across not only the perfect makeshift weapon partially buried in the pile of junk, but one he was perfectly familiar with as a star athlete at his school… an intact Louisville slugger baseball bat.

The teen spun around with the bat ready to swing as he heard the killer's sinister rendition of a classic Christmas carol continue a few feet away.

"He knows when you've been bad or good… but he's gonna kill you just the same! Yeah, I know that isn't how the song goes, but my version is much more appropriate, don't you think?"

Those were Virgil's words as he walked into view of Jake Oliver with the police baton in one hand and the bloody kitchen knife in the other.

"Ohhh, I see the kid found a bat," Virgil mocked. "Are you gonna hit poor old Santa with that?"

"You motherfucking murderer!" Jake bellowed in rage as he charged Virgil.

The serial killer swung the hardwood baton and blocked the plunge of the bat. He then swung back at Jake, whose athletic young form was lithe enough to dodge it.

"Oh ho! You've got slick moves, kid! Just thought I'd give you some cred before I killed you."

Jake stood his ground and positioned the bat for another strike. "You killed my sister! She didn't do nothing to you! None of us did! Why are you doing this?"

"Um, because I like it. Do I need a reason beyond that? Look, don't you judge me, kid! We both live under a really shitty system that takes a lot more than it gives. And it regularly creates… uh, people like me and all the other bastards that prey on each other in these streets. But I'm the alpha among them!

"And I did your sis a favor! She eventually would have gotten fucked by some asshole and impregnated – is that the scientific word for it? –and then gotten fucked *over* by him; and then spent the rest of her life as a useless drug-addicted single mom who raised another little monster."

"You fucking asshole!"

"Okay, either that or ended up in the hands of a pimp who made a good buck off her while she did nothing but lay on her back for losers who had money to spend. A vicious cycle either way. And I ended it! I spared her that!"

"Noooooo!" the enraged Jake lunged at Virgil, taking several more swings with the bat.

The killer moved with a speed and grace akin to a dancer performing pirouettes, dodging each one. He swung back with his baton, only for Jake to use his reach advantage with the bat to strike the bludgeon out of the killer's hand. Virgil quickly spun around, ducked under another swing from the back, and slashed his target across the rib cage with his knife.

Jake yelped in pain and fell back against the dumpster, one hand instinctively covering his bleeding side. His thick winter coat and the sweater underneath had thankfully prevented the blade from cutting too deep. The tough young athlete pushed through the pain and forced himself back to his feet while readying the bat for another attack.

"You had no reason to hurt us!" Jake hollered as he prepared for another strike.

"I told you, kid! Me and a few others like me are the alpha bastards of a society full of all kinds of bastards," the killer replied as he raised his gleaming knife. "We're part of the clean-up crew of a society that deserves to fall beneath the blades and blows of the bastards it creates. Those of us with no silly emotional buffers like remorse or empathy; and with a love and talent for killing. Or, put another way, those of us who develop the proper tools to do the job and lack the impediments against getting the job done.

"I serve a useful purpose in this society that you could never understand. Why deny me the right to have fun and enjoy myself while doing it?"

"You fucking sick bastard!"

"Well, my psychiatrist agreed with that. It's how he got me a stay of execution in court and sent me to that foolish hospital where I was eventually able to escape from. I did that this very night, in fact. Lucky for you and your poor little siblings to run into me and make my Christmas Eve while I totally fucked up yours!"

"You... asshole!"

Jake charged towards Virgil once again, his fury providing him the fuel to attack with fearsome strength.

The bat swung forth with sufficient power to smash Virgil's skull with a single blow. Unfortunately, Jake's rage caused the swing to go wild and reckless, allowing the Killer Santa to duck under it. The inertia of the swing sent the high school senior moving forward and Virgil took advantage of this by moving in and sinking his blade directly between the boy's ribs. Jake Oliver gasped as he felt his left lung being punctured. He fell onto the ice-covered concrete panting for air and coughing up blood.

Virgil put his knife into a pocket on his red coat and picked up Jake's discarded baseball bat. He hovered the wooden club above the teen as his body underwent shock-induced spasms. Jake still seemed conscious and aware, however.

"Are you still with me, kid?" Virgil queried with a kick to the teen's side.

"Fuck… fuck you," Jake sputtered defiantly along with another oral expulsion of blood.

"Sorry, kid. You fought well, but you're not the alpha here. And I'm doing *you* a favor, too. If you had some dreams of being a pro athlete, forget that shit. Your chances were slim against all the competition.

"Much more likely you would have just parlayed your good looks into fathering who knows how many kids, all of which would have grown up under conditions to produce the next generation of drug dealers and gang bangers killing each other and everyone around them to turn a profit. Or petty crooks spending most of their lives filling a prison cell. Or… maybe one of them would have won the bastard lottery to become the next *me.*"

"Fuck… you…"

"Go ahead and be that way. But thank you for this awesome Christmas gift, kid. And here's my gift to you… an end to the life of misery you would have had."

The Killer Santa raised the bat and brought it down several times on Jake's face, smashing its handsome features into a mass of blood-soaked pulp.

Upon finishing the deadly deed, Virgil walked out of the parking lot to see another young boy run past the end of the block in seemingly mortal terror. It quickly became apparent that he was the same little boy that had walked past Virgil in the company of the former's mom earlier that night in front of the Salvation Army center.

*Well, well… it seems like Christmas Eve keeps on giving! I got another chance at that little pipsqueak. But it seems like someone else is after him too, and whoever it is, he seems to have gotten the boy's mom. Ah well. At least I have the chance to get one of the two again. And after being in that parking lot, I could see exactly the short cut I can take to head that tyke off.*

"Wait up, boy!" Virgil shouted aloud as he raised the bat and ran into the parking lot towards the short cut he noticed. "Santa Claus is coming, and he has the perfect gift for you! Hah! Hah!"

## END

# SILVER AND MOLD

Linda Laughton was not keen on having a séance in Forest Hill Cemetery on Christmas Eve. However, three of her newest friends from Detroit Community College – Jennifer, Megan, and Tipsy – were urging her to take a go at it. It was their opinion that such an act of Spiritualism was the best way she could achieve closure for a horrifically tragic event in her childhood – one related to a previous trip to Forest Hill on a snowy Christmas Eve ten years previous. That incident was nothing less than the mysterious disappearance of her childhood friend Carol Anne Nellis. This occurred when the two adventurous nine-year-olds ventured into the darkness of the graveyard to hold a séance of their own.

*\*\*\**

Christmas Eve circa 1967 seemed like a festive night despite the bitter cold on Detroit's West Side. Many people stood outside their doors that holiday evening on Meyers Avenue where best friends Linda and Carol Anne grew up together. These good neighbors stood in front of a twelve-foot communal Christmas tree while singing carols and listening to the seasonal songs playing on their transistor radios courtesy of many local stations. The chill of the night was no bother, as shared thermoses of hot cocoa and holiday cheer helped warm them up.

Linda sat on the front steps of the modest apartment building she cohabited with her single mom listening to the festivities. She wanted to be happy and join in, but the recent loss of her beloved grandfather hung over her like an appalling pall.

Her depression was given a bit of relief when her best bud Carol Anne, who was part of the caroling group, turned around and saw her friend sitting alone in a state of melancholy. Always on hand to offer a shoulder when needed, and knowing exactly what was wrong, Carol Anne broke off from the festive ensemble and ran to sit next to Linda.

"Sitting here like a Gloomy Gus is not gonna bring him back, Linds," she said after giving her friend a compassionate shoulder pat. "I think he would've wanted you to sing and remember the good times you had together. Especially on Christmas Eve."

"No," Linda said as she began to shed tears. "The family get-togethers over the holidays will never be the same without him. No one liked Christmas as much as he did. My mom and my aunt sure as heck don't. All they want to do tomorrow is watch some TV together and that's it."

"Aww. Look, I have an idea on how you can contact your grandpa, see that he's okay, and have him tell you to keep the Christmas spirit going for him. Even though it's... well, kinda a crazy idea."

Linda wiped her teary eyes on the sleeve of her heavy woolen coat. "Tell me."

"Well... I've been using the Ouija board my Aunt Boon got me for my birthday last summer. I've learned a few things."

"Carol Anne! You know I don't like that thing. I don't wanna use it. Especially not on Christmas Eve!"

"Look, we won't have the privacy in my house to do it anyways. I learned enough to talk to spirits without the board and that creepy moving scope. So, I'm saying we should go to the cemetery up the street where your grandad is buried and have a séance in front of his tombstone. Let's get him to appear so you can talk to him, if only for a few minutes. We just need a few things connected to him to make that happen. His stone will be one of them."

"Oh god, no! Carol Anne, that is really trippy! I'm not gonna do that! If he did show up, I-I'd be too freaked out to say a single word! I might even run or faint, or something like that. And... I don't wanna offend him or anything."

Christofer Nigro
*Silver and Mold*
Yuletide Horrors Volume 1


"Don't worry. I'll be the – what's the word? – the *mediator.* Yea, that's it. I'll make sure that all goes smoothly."

Linda put both her hands over her face. "I-I dunno. But I miss him so much. And it's Christmas Eve. If he was still with us, he would be here right now, leading those people in the singing…"

Carol Anne gently took her grieving friend's hand. "It's gonna be okay. I'll be there. I won't let'cha down, just like I know you would never let *me* down. Now, do you have anything of his that might help us reach out? The cemetery is a place full of power, and on the eve of Christmas, it's *super-powerful!* I'm telling you; we can do this."

"I-I have this that he gave me about a year ago for Christmas."

Linda reached into her pocket and produced a shiny coin with the head of St. Nicholas in place of any president's image. Its color was divided into silver and gold, two shades that classically symbolized the season.

"That's perfect! So, c'mon, let's go before it gets any later and people start going inside and our moms make us go indoors too."

Linda had always trusted Carol Anne, so within moments the girls were striding down the two blocks leading to Forest Hill Cemetery on the corner of Meyers and Lyndon. The gates were locked, but the bars were just wide enough for the determined duo to slip through.

As requested, Linda led Carol Anne through the snow-covered bushes and multitude of tombstones towards where the Earthly remains of the former's granddad had been interred. The merry singing of the neighbors could no longer be heard at this distance, and the entire graveyard was eerily silent save for the occasional tree branch rustling in the chill winter wind. The drifting snow gave the appearance of a murky mist enveloping the dark landscape, as if a thousand large cubes of dry ice had been dumped into the local stream.

When Linda could no longer tolerate the deafening silence, she reached into her coat pocket and pulled out her small Imperial transistor radio. She clicked it on and began shuffling through AM stations, with snippets of "I'm a Believer" by the Monkees and "He's a Loser" by the Mosquitos suddenly filling the chilly atmosphere with incongruous music.

Carol Anne immediately turned to her friend. "Linds, what are you doing?"

"This place was too quiet," Linda replied. "It was scaring me. Can't we listen to some music while we do this?"

"No. It has to be silent so I can concentrate. Sorry, but you gotta turn off the radio."

Linda exhaled in frustration. "Oh, c'mon! You gotta love the Mosquitos! Irving is so dreamy!"

"Actually, I prefer Bongo. He's the grooviest of the bunch, with those eyes… and that hair! But… I really gotta have quiet while I do this, Linds. This is serious stuff, and I don't want anything to go wrong."

Linda gave a flustered groan but complied.

"Don't be scared. I'm here, so you got nothing at all to worry about."

"Carol Anne, if this kinda stuff is so serious… maybe we shouldn't take the chance of doing it."

"It'll be okay, I know what I'm doing. And we're already here, so let's not chicken out and waste this chance. Besides, I really wanna see if I can do this like I think I can."

The two of them soon reached the marble sepulcher of Gerald Laughton. Linda struggled against breaking out in tears.

"Hi, grandpa," she said softly.

Carol Anne reached out her hand. "Okay, let's do this. Gimme that coin."

Linda grudgingly did as requested. Her best friend then bowed her head down while holding up both arms, including the hand holding the precious coin gifted to Linda by her grandad. Carol Anne recited a few brief lines in a potent, no-nonsense tone of voice demanding that the necromantic energies of the location couple with the seasonal Yuletide forces to compel the shade of Gerold Laughton to materialize in front of them.

Nothing happened. Even after they waited, shivering in the cold, for several minutes… nothing.

"Oh… crap," Carol Anne griped softly.

"Don't let my mom ever hear you use language like that," Linda reminded her. "Or, she won't let us hang anymore."

"It didn't happen. I could swear I felt… something. But no. I guess not." She sighed loudly. "I'm sorry I dragged you here for nothing, Linds. Let's just go."

The two girls began trudging through the snowy earth towards the front gate of Forest Hill, both eager to leave that area with due haste. They were wary of slipping on the ice and possibly enduring a broken bone, however.

As they walked on top of a knoll about fifty feet from the front gates, they saw two older boys they knew as upperclassmen from the local high school walking past the front gate. The lads spotted the girls and one of the boys spoke to them.

"Yo! Is that you up there, Carol Anne?"

"Yea, it's me, Frankie," she replied.

"What in God's name are you doing in this place? Why aren't you celebrating the holidays on your street instead?"

"I just thought it would be a gas to visit this place at night with my friend Linda."

"Oh, hi there, Linda… Laughton, right?" the other boy queried as he waved. "I used to deliver the newspaper to your house, remember?"

"Yea, I remember you, Darryl," Linda confirmed. "How've you been?"

"I just graduated, so I've been fabulous," Darryl replied with a smile. "Say, it's pretty dark now. We can walk you girls home. I actually think we should."

"Nah, it's only like two blocks away," Carol Anne answered for them both. "We'll be fine."

"Suit yourself," Frankie answered. "You girls take care."

The two pairs said a quick goodbye and the boys walked on, disappearing into the shadows on the left side of the front gate.

"Aren't they far-out?" Carol Anne asked in a swooning tone. "Especially Frankie?"

"If you say so," Linda rejoined with a slight tone of sarcasm. "Can we just get out of here now?"

The duo were given a sudden start when they heard a loud barking sound coming from straight ahead. They looked through the bars of the front gate to see a large dog strutting by and looking straight ahead, almost as if trying to catch up to Frankie and Darryl.

"Geez Louise, that dog was big!" Carol Anne exclaimed.

"Maybe we shouldn't go out there just yet?" Linda wondered.

"We'll be fine. I'm pretty sure that was the Chocolate Lab that belongs to Frankie's neighbors. He's harmless and they let him run around loose all night sometimes. He's probably following the boys 'cause he knows Frankie, who used to feed him and stuff. C'mon, let's get moving. Just be careful going down this hill, it's really slippery."

Both the girls began moving down the snow-covered mound with care. Then, suddenly, Carol Anne began inexplicably picking up speed and rushing down the hillock with greater haste, as if no longer caring about the weather conditions.

"Carol Anne, slow down! You tell me to be careful, but now look at you!"

Her friend continued moving at the faster pace, finally reaching the bottom and turning a corner leading to the first section of the front gate, which was not visible from Linda's vantage point.

"Carol Anne! Wait up, okay?"

Linda then similarly picked up her own pace and reached the bottom of the hill safely in just a few seconds. She turned the corner to find that Carol Anne was nowhere in sight. She called to her, but her friend did not answer.

Linda assumed that her friend had slipped through the bars of the front gate and was waiting for her a few feet up the street, near where the two boys and the dog had gone. If so, why wouldn't she answer when called? It was clearly in earshot of Linda's voice.

She slipped through the bars and looked in both directions on the street. Carol Anne was nowhere. The block was only visible in each direction for about ten feet before the rest was swallowed up with a combination of shadows and blowing snow.

"Carol Anne! Where are you?"

Now beginning to panic, Linda tried another tactic. "Frankie! Darryl! Are you still there?"

Nothing from them either. The street was eerily quiet, with no sign of movement save for swirling snowflakes and tree branches swaying slightly in the wind.

Finally, the panic took over completely and Linda began running up the left side of the block, leading away from the cemetery and towards Meyer Avenue where both girls lived just two blocks away. Her fast sprint was paused only for about thirty seconds when she slipped on the ice and banged up her knee. She quickly catered to the bloody scrape visible through her torn blue jeans and continued running.

"Carol Anne! Where are you? Please answer me! Stop fooling around, this isn't funny!"

Linda Laughton continued screaming all the way back home. The hysterically crying girl quickly caught the attention of the caroling neighbors – among them, Carol Anne's mother – when she reached Meyer Avenue fifteen minutes later. It took over ten minutes for the group of no longer festive adults and kids to calm her down enough to talk, including with the aid of her mother, Susan. By then, Carol Anne's mother was likewise hysterical.

Carol Anne was never found despite a massive search by the local police that was joined by the local Boy Scouts and a thousand civilian volunteers. No evidence of what had happened to her was ever found, either. Numerous people were interviewed, including Frankie and Darryl. They both insisted they had turned onto another block to bring home a neighbors' runaway dog before Carol Anne ever left the cemetery's front gates – assuming that she did. A few months later, both young men moved to different states.

After sufficiently regaining her composure days later, Carol Anne's mother approached Linda and assured her that she didn't blame her for the loss of her daughter and believed her allegations that it was Carol Anne's idea to go to the cemetery that ill-fated Christmas Eve. Subsequently, Linda only rarely saw the woman who had become like a second mother to her over the following year, after which she also moved out of state and never kept in touch.

Linda and the community attempted to go on with their lives as best they could. After about a year, it appeared as if they were successfully doing so, despite the local papers continuing to periodically mention the strange and tragic unsolved disappearance and the police never truly closing the investigation.

But Linda never forgot the loss, and the image of Carol Anne – with her pale blue eyes and dark blonde, almost shoulder-length Flipped Bob hairstyle – never left her mind, where it was indelibly frozen in time. It became harder than ever to forget over the next ten years whenever Christmas Eve arrived, as that season reminded Linda of two losses that she would never get over.

***

Jump back ahead ten years, as Linda's three friends were trying to get her to repeat history.

"C'mon, Linda," badgered Jennifer, the frequent leader of their little circle. "You need some closure on this! You haven't been back to that cemetery since then. Maybe we can find some trace of what happened to Carol Anne."

"I think you're crazy, Jen!" Linda retorted. "I do want to find out what happened to her! Carol Anne's vanishing has tortured me all these years! But it's a ten-year-old cold case! How the hell can you expect to find a clue that might lead to solving a disappearance that happened so long ago? Especially when hundreds of people, including the entire DPD and any number of private investigators Mrs. Nellis hired, couldn't find a goddamned thing?"

"What you're not understanding here because of your grief, however understandable," Megan interjected as gently as she could manage, "is that new investigations of vintage cold cases can offer new perspectives that may not have occurred to the investigators back then. You just gotta try to think positively about it."

"I think it's you who doesn't understand!" Linda shouted. "This whole thing still weighs on me, and it's been getting worse, not better, as time goes on. And it's worse than ever on Christmas Eve! I swear I can feel her then."

"And it's Christmas Eve tomorrow night," Megan reminded her dark-haired friend. "I think it'll be really cool to do an investigation for that reason if nothing else! We'll be like a foursome of Nancy Drews! Or, one of those other teen sleuth teams you read about, like Mystery, Inc., the Bloodhound Gang, those Clue Clubbers – and that other crew with a dog, the weird ass one who claims their pooch turns invisible or some shit like that when he gets all 'fraidy; the crew that one of those groups of singing kid siblings hangs around with for some reason. You know the one I'm talking about, right?"

"You think this is all fun and games, don't you?" Linda spat at Megan with severe vitriol. "Carol Anne was my best friend! If I had argued harder against going to that goddamned cemetery, she might still be here, hanging out with us right now! Then you would have known her too, and understood firsthand what a good friend she was!"

"Calm down, I'm sorry," Megan lamented with a very gentle tone. "I just... I mean, I just think it's sorta fascinating. I know what happened is horrible, and very upsetting to you. But... what if we can crack this case?"

"Right now, Megan, I feel more like cracking your fucking head!" Linda rejoined.

"Easy, easy," Jennifer said as she put her arms between the two to form a barrier.

The soft-spoken redhead Tipsy simply took a few steps back, fearful to interject with any words of her own and more than content to let Jennifer handle this volatile situation.

"Look," Jennifer calmly began explaining. "I know Megan may sound selfish, but she is correct in essence, Linda."

"What do you mean by that?" Linda enquired.

"Well, I think it would benefit you, and the entire community, if we could find a clue as to what happened to your friend." Jennifer was clearly choosing her words carefully, while still playing the leader of the pack. "Megan and I have done lots of research on true crime, which isn't hard to come by when you live in *this* city."

"Jen, ten years ago not only did the whole DPD comb that cemetery from one end to the other, but so did the Boy Scouts, the caretakers of the place, and about a few million local volunteers," Linda explicated with a tinge of hyperbole. "They found nada. In fact, we can't even be certain that Carol Anne was a victim of any sort of foul play. We just don't know what happened to her."

"Of *course,* she was a victim of foul play!" Megan interjected.

"How can you possibly know that, Meg?" Linda asked the would-be sleuth.

"Think about it," Megan entreated, trying to hide any sign of enthusiasm in her voice. "You said there was no chance she had simply run away and had planned that whole trip to the cemetery under your nose. So, I'm thinking she was abducted and murdered by those two boys from Lyndon Street that were outside the front gate. The ones you said offered to walk the two of you home. It's a good thing your friend ran on ahead of you."

"Frankie and Darryl?" Linda glared at her friend. "There is no way to be certain. The cops questioned and investigated them. There was no evidence, and they had no criminal records."

"How about since then?" Megan queried.

"I don't know," Linda responded honestly. "It's hard to check that sort of stuff. I have no idea what ever happened to either of them when they moved out of state. I never heard anything about them in the national news, though. When that awful serial killer Virgil Kennedy went on a rampage in this city six years ago, it wasn't only reported here, but in papers all over the fucking world. So, we should have heard something about Frankie and Darryl if they turned out to be killers."

"I think that big ass dog you two saw before Carol Anne left the cemetery is responsible," Jennifer conjectured. "It probably dragged her off and ate her or something. There are some seriously dangerous mutant dogs out there. I read about something called the Jack Dog running around and killing people in Buffalo, New York last summer. It's crazy, but it happens!"

"But Carol Anne thought she recognized the dog," Linda pointed out. "She said it was harmless and that it was just following Frankie. And if it was like that Jack Dog you mentioned, how come there were no reports before or since of a killer dog in Detroit?"

Tipsy remained quiet and turned to Jennifer, awaiting her reply.

"Like I said, there are too many unanswered questions," Megan opined, "and things that may or may not be clues. We need to investigate this ourselves. And we need to do it tomorrow night, on Christmas Eve, to commemorate the loss you suffered."

"I don't want to go near that fucking place," Linda insisted. "Ever again."

"We understand," Jennifer gently replied. "But, not for nothing, Linda... I think you owe it to Carol Anne to find out what happened to her. And you owe it to yourself to confront that place, on the night in question, to move past your fears of facing up to this. The three of us will be there for you, and we'll help you figure this out."

Linda did not want to do this, but Jennifer was persuasive. Megan was determined and backed up the group leader. Tipsy was quiet, but her tendency to just go along with Jennifer somehow seemed to help encourage others to do so as well.

"Okay," Linda said. "Let's do this."

Jennifer smiled, Tipsy smiled in solidarity with her; and Megan did her best to bite her tongue and conceal her triumphant excitement.

***

Christmas Eve came, as it did every year, and like each year for the past ten, it was not a cause of celebration for Linda Laughton. There were too many horrible memories attached to it. This year, her friends Jennifer and Megan, would celebrate in a different way than usual. Their interest in making a rep for themselves as amateur crime investigators so they could possibly earn a scholarship into one of the nation's best universities to study their chosen art was their way of giving a gift to themselves. Tipsy, who simply wanted to belong, was, as always, along for any ride that the beautiful and popular 19-year-old Jennifer took her on.

Once Jennifer and Megan met Linda at the local community college, they considered it the equivalent of a Miner 49er striking gold. She was the key witness and participant in one of Detroit's most baffling unsolved vanishings, and they were determined to use her to discover clues to what really happened to Carol Anne Nellis ten years ago. If it truly ended up helping Linda and others achieve a sense of closure... well, that would be great, as fringe benefits abound in this job.

Linda cringed as she entered Forest Hill Cemetery for the first time in ten years. Like before, she did so on a cold Christmas Eve night when more sane people would be at home enjoying a cup of cocoa with the family and anticipating the joys of a family gathering the following day. As before, she wasn't entering the place alone – only this time with three others whom she considered peripheral albeit influential friends, rather than only one who she considered the best friend she ever had.

And like before, the graveyard was quiet with drifts of snow that created the appearance of a fog-shrouded land of the dead that it truly was. The landscape and atmosphere were simultaneously serene and disquieting.

The girls were no longer quite thin enough to slip through the bars of the front gates, so Jennifer used some skills she acquired to pick the lock. As they entered, Megan pulled out a small pocket cassette recorder and began dictating a report.

"We're here. We're actually here! Me, Jen, and the actual witness to the crime we're investigating, Linda Laughton! And, um, yea, Tipsy is with us too. The cemetery looks so radically spooky on this Christmas Eve. No sounds of caroling, not even from any spirits. No decorations adorned with flashing lights, no trees to show off the decorative skills of the owners. No steaming cups of hot chocolate to relieve the bitter cold. Just four girls in the valley of tombstones, investigating the unknown in the hope of finally finding the answers to a tragic disappearance that the city has never gotten over."

Megan continued: "Carol Anne Nellis... what happened to you? That is what *we* are here to find out."

Jennifer could not help but roll her eyes. "Oh, Megan, cut down on the melodrama and the cheese, would ya?" she said quietly.

Linda merely looked around and closed her eyes. Tears began flowing as familiar sights began triggering the memories of that night. *Yes, Carol Anne, my dearest friend. What happened to you? I hate this, but if there's any chance these girls can help me find out...*

The group was surprised when the usually silent Tipsy suddenly spoke. "Look what I just found!"

The others ran over to her and looked down at a bare spot in the snow where Tipsy pointed. The girl then bent down and picked up a small object.

"It looks like a quarter, but with the head of some guy with a big hat I don't think any president ever wore. Half of it is silver, but the other half looks like it used to be gold or copper, but it's now greenish, like it became all moldy."

Linda's eyes suddenly popped wide. "Oh my god! That's... that's the coin my grandfather gave me during his final Christmas with us! Carol Anne still had it when she... disappeared. It was laying here all this time? But why didn't any of the cops and other investigators over the years come across it?"

The other three girls looked at the coin in Tipsy's palm with quizzical expressions.

"Are you sure that's it?" Megan asked.

"Yes, I'm sure!" Linda replied. "Let me have it..."

Tipsy uncharacteristically closed her hand and raised her arm high. "No, I found it! Do I get the credit? Do I...?"

That was the moment when the horror began. Tipsy suddenly turned around to see standing near one of the sepulchers what looked like a young girl wearing ragged winter clothes indicative of a decade earlier. Her roughly shoulder-length hair was straggly and greasy but looked as it may once have been a dark blonde. The girl then slowly, almost mechanically turned around to reveal that her face was a deathly alabaster white. Her lips and eyes were dark black, with the latter showing no sign of pupils; it was as if the iris had grown and taken over the entire lens.

The mysterious and terrifying girl smiled what looked to be a sinister grin, revealing yellowed but straight teeth.

"Hello, Linda," she said in an echoey voice that otherwise appeared startlingly familiar.

"Oh my... god," Linda rambled. "Carol Anne?"

"It can't be..." Jennifer responded.

"Jen..." the trembling Megan drawled out. "Whoever that girl is... there's something *seriously fucked up* about her. Just looking at her is making me freak the fuck out!"

Just then, the apparition purporting to be that of Carol Anne Nellis opened her mouth into a large "O" shape and began emitting a piercing sound. The emanations were directed at Jennifer and Megan, who covered their ears in a futile attempt to drown out the debilitating waves of sound. They fell to the snowy ground, their eardrums feeling as if they were on fire; and their minds filled with terrifying imagery. The girls screamed like they never had before as the images of their greatest fears and most unpleasant real life experiences assailed their psyches in magnified form.

Carol Anne looked up and swooned with an expression of orgasmic pleasure. It was as if the extreme terror she was causing the girls to emote were being absorbed by her like it was the nectar of the gods.

Tipsy simply stood transfixed, seemingly too terrified to move a muscle.

Linda shouted, "Carol Anne! If that is really you, please stop! Please! *You're hurting them!"*

Carol Anne turned to look at her one-time best friend as the latter called out to her. The apparition's blackened lips then slid from an ecstatic smile to an angered sneer. In a flash of motion, Carol Anne appeared to rise a few inches off the ground and fly in a standing position towards Tipsy, the holder of the coin. The phantom girl covered the physical distance in what looked to be a quick blur of motion to the human eye, and her spectral form seemed to enter Tipsy's body.

Tipsy then turned to look at Linda, who was standing just a few feet away. To Linda's horror, Tipsy now had the dark black eyes she saw in Carol Anne's spectre, with her lips pulled down in the same type of enraged smirk. Now having access to a physical body, the mad ghost maneuvered Tipsy into grasping Linda by the throat and easily slamming her into a huge tombstone. The possessed girl's strength was immense, and Linda choked and gagged as she desperately struggled to break the grip that was rapidly strangling her to death.

"Why, Linda?" the possessed Tipsy asked her. "Why did you leave me here? How could you let it happen to me?"

"I... don't know what... happened to you, Carol Anne," Linda managed to get out between gasps for air. "I didn't... see. I swear. I would have done... anything to help you. I... loved you like a sister. I... still do. Please stop."

"Liar!" Carol Anne screeched angrily through Tipsy's vocal chords as she caused host's possessed body to slam Linda against the marble sepulcher again. "You left me! You let... that happen to me! You coward! You... rotten traitor of a friend! *You let me down!"*

What Carol Anne failed to consider in her rage, however, was that possessing a physical form caused the effects of her "spirit scream" to fade. Jennifer and Megan recovered and did their best to shake the lingering, traumatic effects of having their greatest fears and worst experiences projected into their minds like a flooding cascade.

"Megan, we have to get her off Linda!" Jennifer yelled.

"Seriously?" Megan replied. "We gotta get the fuck out of here while we can, is what we gotta do!"

"Listen! We talked her into coming here, so we're responsible! And we gotta help Tipsy too!"

Never one to go against Jennifer, even in a situation like this, Megan joined her friend in charging at the possessed Tipsy. They both grabbed the young woman and struggled to pull her arm from Linda's throat before she succumbed to strangulation or a crushed trachea. Jennifer wrapped both her arms around the possessed Tipsy's forearm and struggled to yank it off Linda even as the latter did the same, while Megan pounded Carol Anne's host furiously in her kidneys and stomach.

"Sorry, Tips," she said quietly.

Though the strength enhancement effect of any host Carol Anne possessed could resist this punishment, at least for a while, it still triggered the host's pain receptors… which the apparition could now feel herself. This enabled Linda to finally break free of her grasp. The ghostly girl then had Tipsy swat Jennifer in the face, sending her careening through the air several yards to land hard on a pile of snow. Consciousness was quick to slip away.

"You bitch!" Megan screamed as she picked up a chunk of ice and slammed Tipsy in the head twice.

The twin blows gave Tipsy a concussion, and the pain was sufficient to cause Carol Anne to vacate the host. The former's extricated body collapsed unconscious to the snow-shrouded ground. The coin fell onto a slab of stone beside her.

Then, with a scream of rage, Megan hurled the ice chunk at the still visible apparition, but it passed right through her immaterial form without causing any damage. Carol Anne's spectre gritted her yellowish teeth at her attacker, first in an expression suggesting amusement but quickly becoming something more akin to anger.

"Experience terror," the ghost said as she again sent her piercing wail at Megan.

The target collapsed into a kicking and screaming heap as her mind was besieged all at once by the worst nightmares that ever plagued her subconscious, along with amplified versions of several she had experienced in real life. Carol Anne again smiled as she drank in the flavorful emotions generated by her victim's terror.

"Carol Anne, stop it!" the newly recovered Linda screeched. "You need to stop it!"

"No, I do not," was all the smiling apparition would say in response. "I'll get back to you for abandoning me after I've had my feeding."

"I didn't abandon you, damn it! I swear I have no idea what happened to you!"

For a moment, Linda felt helpless, as she realized that she was incapable of physically attacking and stopping the intangible ghost from tormenting Megan. Then she caught sight of the coin laying on the base of one of the tombstones and remembered the role it seemed to play in being the catalyst for Carol Anne's manifestation and her ability to possess another.

Linda snatched up the metal object and raised her hand in a throwing position.

"Carol Anne! I know you're connected somehow to my grandpa's coin! Stop what you're doing, or I swear I'll throw it far away! It will send you back to whatever hell you've been to for the past ten years!"

The apparition ceased her spiritual attack on Megan and turned to her former best friend.

"Noooo! You won't!"

"I'm sorry, but I have to! I want to help you more than anything, Carol Anne! I honestly don't know what happened to you, but you died and became some kind of monster! And you won't listen to me! I'm sorry! I'm sorry all over again!"

"Nooooo! I won't let you!"

The apparition again elevated herself from the ground and flew towards Linda in the blink of an eye, since she held the coin. This happened just as

Linda began to throw it. The end result was a flashing portal surrounding the two that transported both the twisted ghost of one girl and a still living one miles outside of the cemetery.

Left behind were three wannabe sleuths who would recover with a very unbelievable story to tell. The greatest shame was that no one would believe them.

## EPILOGUE

Linda Laughton found herself out of breath but otherwise unharmed. The chilly night air helped her regain her senses rather quickly. She looked around to see she that was no longer inside Forest Hill Cemetery but was outside a decrepit apartment complex that she recognized as being on Detroit's Far East Side.

Apparently, she was subjected to some type of teleportation effect when she attempted to throw the coin at the same time Carol Anne's ghost made contact with her.

Suddenly she was alerted to what sounded like frantic huffing and puffing coming from the parking lot stretching into the adjacent apartment complex. She soon beheld its source as an African American youth of about ten years of age tottered out from the multi-car driveway on a single crutch that looked as if it had just been taken from the garbage. His right leg had a serious wound, and just above it a scarf was tied tightly to control the blood loss.

The boy shuffled onto the sidewalk where Linda was laying, and he turned as he noticed her. Even though the youth was obviously in a lot of pain and seemed heavily traumatized by whatever had caused his injury, he still instinctively reached out to her.

"Lady… are you okay?"

"I'm fine. And my name is Linda Laughton. But, you…"

"Hi… Linda. I'm Lem Oliver. And… I've been shot by some crazy man. We've… gotta get out of here."

"I'll try and help you."

That was when something on the sidewalk a few inches from Lem's foot caught his attention.

"What's... that?"

As he began reaching for the object, Linda looked at it and realized, to her horror, that it was the silver and gold coin she now realized must have contained Carol Anne's ghostly essence.

"No, Lem! Don't pick that up!"

But it was too late...

## END

# THE YULETIDE MASSACRE MELEE

Linda Laughton was not very happy on Christmas Eve circa 1977. She just had a harrowing experience on the opposite end of Detroit in Forest Hill Cemetery. There she and a trio of friends went to search for any clues that may lead to the answer of how her best childhood friend, Carol Anne Nellis, mysteriously disappeared there ten years previous. The end result of that excursion into the unknown was finding a battered, mold-encrusted coin that was given to Linda by her grandfather the Christmas before he died – and which Carol Anne had in her hand when she vanished following a séance in an attempt to summon the deceased man's spirit in front of his gravesite.

Carol Anne appeared in the graveyard as soon as one of Linda's friends mysteriously found the coin and picked it up. Only she was no longer alive, and she was not just any type of ghost; she was a *hungry ghost,* one seeking to induce fear in others and feed upon the emotional residue resulting from the terror. She also blamed Linda for not saving her from whatever took her from this world years earlier – something Linda was genuinely not in the know about, which is something the enraged ghostly girl seemed unable to accept.

To make a long story (or, more specifically, three short stories) shorter, that evening saw a convergence of three deadly beings appearing in Detroit, one of them the aforementioned *hungry ghost,* and also a man-eating, shape-shifting Hindu demon known as a *rakshasa* and a psychotic *alpha serial killer* named Virgil Kennedy, who had just escaped from a

51

mental hospital. During the conflagration in the cemetery, Carol Anne used the coin to transport herself and Linda to the Far East Side of Detroit, where both the rakshasa and Kennedy were wreaking bloody havoc on various targets.

Little were these victims – as well as the predatory demon, alpha serial killer, and hungry ghost girl – aware that their paths were about to converge in a deadly three-way fight to the finish.

\*\*\*

No sooner was she transported there, then she regained consciousness to find out that a tall twelve-year-old youth named Lem, who was trying to escape from Kennedy after being shot in the leg by him, stumbled upon the discarded coin which contained Carol Anne's essence and was in the process of picking it up.

"Lem! Drop that coin, now!" Linda exclaimed as she jumped to her feet to knock it out of his hand.

Her hopes were dashed as the boy looked up at her with a sadistic grin and eyes that were suddenly opaque black. He was now possessed by the twisted ghost of Carol Anne Nellis.

"Hi, again, Linda," she said through Lem's larynx. "Did you think you could stop me from punishing you for abandoning me at the cemetery ten years ago?"

"I didn't leave you behind on purpose, Carol Anne! You must believe me that I didn't see what happened to you! You just disappeared after you ran down that hill before I could catch up with you!"

"Bull hockey! You had to have seen what happened! You—"

Just then, Carol Anne was cut off as she stumbled when the pain of Lem's bullet-riddled leg hit her at full force.

"Eeeaaa! This body's leg hurts!"

"He's been shot! You need to leave that body now and go back into the coin. I'll try to figure out with happened to you and help you pass over—"

"Shut up! And nice try. I'm—I'm just gonna have to... use some energy to fix this body up a bit. I took lots of it from your friends back at the cemetery when I made them experience terror. It's soooo good to be out of that cemetery, at least!"

It was then that Carol Anne focused the emotional energies she stole in abundance from Linda's two friends Jennifer and Megan back at Forest Hill. She forcibly projected some excess power into the shattered leg of her host body. Within seconds, right before Linda's awestruck eyes, the cracked bone began knitting together and the flesh started healing in a circular pattern. Lem's voice yelped as the physically painful process ensued, which had to be consciously forced by Carol Anne's mind every step of the way. And she had to experience every unpleasant physical sensation that her hosts' nerve endings did when she took possession of one.

It took just under a minute, and the gaping leg wound was reduced to a small, quarter-sized hole in the flesh. It still hurt, but the fractured bone and ruptured vessels were fixed so no more blood loss was occurring. She also managed to replenish most of the corpuscles and oxygen that her host had lost.

Lem's body slumped over while struggling to catch his breath when the deed was done as well as it could be done by the extra energies Carol Anne's ghost had available to her. Obviously, the most severe types of wounds could not be healed, and a dead body was no good as a host. And if one was killed outright or cut to pieces, the ghost girl was likely S.O.L. She would be forced to leave that body and attack in the non-physical ways her incorporeal form allowed.

"I'm going to have to take more energy if I want to be able to do this again soon," Carol Anne mused as Lem's body recovered from the ordeal.

"Carol Anne, please don't."

"I said, shut up! You and me are now gonna have *words,* ex-friend. And this time there's no one around to pull me off when I'm smashing the answers out of you..."

"Hey, hey, so look who I found?" came a soft but somehow sinister voice from behind them.

Linda and the possessed Lem turned to see a smiling man wearing a Santa Claus suit... who also happened to be holding a baseball bat smeared with blood. Linda winced right away, realizing this must have been the man who shot Lem.

"Before I wade into you, kid, I thought I would let you know that your brother lost the fight with me," Virgil Kennedy said with a proud smirk visible beneath the false white beard. "Parts of his face are all over the bat here. The one I'm going to use to give you a good old Christmas thrashing. Then I'll move onto that pretty little friend you seem to have made. I'm gonna take my time with her. This is gonna be one fucking hell of a holiday celebration! Well, for me, anyway. Hah! Hah!"

Linda backed away in revulsion, but to Virgil's surprise, Lem did no such thing. He didn't even react to the news that his heroic brother had been killed by this man, the one who first shot and killed his sister, then shot him before killing his brother with the bat. And here he was now, boasting about how he was about to brutally end *his* life. It was then that the serial killer noticed the strange nature of his victim's eyes.

"There's... something different about you, kid," Virgil noted. "Something wicked. I can relate, and I love it. But I'm still gonna kill you."

"Get out of here, Mister Fake Santa," Carol Anne said through Lem's voice. "This is not your concern. Leave here or I'll hurt you."

"Hah! Hah! Really now, kid?" Virgil scoffed. "I see whatever weird shit happened to you gave you a shot of courage... or is that foolishness? Let's see who hurts who right now!"

The Killer Santa let out a bellow of rage as he raised the bat and charged at the possessed Lem.

Linda jumped to the side of a snowbank. "Carol Anne, don't let Lem get hurt!"

At first, the ghostly girl was taken by surprise with the sheer savagery of the man's attack. Carol Anne knew that any good blow in the right place that is either unexpectedly painful or which causes severe damage could make her etheric form spontaneously vacate the host. She was thus determined to use the body's now enhanced reflexes and strength to protect all vital areas as best she could.

She managed to use Lem's arms to block Virgil's first swing of the bat. The blow hurt, though not badly enough to cause sufficient pain or damage to force her ghostly essence out of his body. She also managed to swat away his second swing, barely managing to deflect it from smashing Lem's skull. The unliving girl knew that she could not keep this up for long, as this man, whoever he may be, was proving himself to be vicious, lacking any inhibitions against inflicting lethal damage, and worst of all, *fast* and quite adept at using homicidal force.

*I gotta end this now. Before Linda gets away because of this creep who likes dressing as Santa.*

"You're good, kid!" Virgil admitted. "But no matter what the hell weird thing happened to you in the last few minutes, you're never gonna be better than me!"

Virgil endeavored to back up that boast with another deadly swing of the bat. This time, however, his brag fell short as Lem caught the makeshift bludgeon in his hands. The grip of the boy's fingers was so strong that the serial killer found himself unable to yank the club free.

That was because a side effect of the possession process endows the host body with incredible strength that trickles well into the superhuman range. Carol Anne put that to use by having Lem turn the tables on Virgil; using his tight hold on the bat to whirl the killer around in the air and then releasing the cudgel to send him flying twenty feet away. The Santa-garbed killer yelled in surprise while he was airborne and slammed into the mortar wall of the tenement building across the street. He slumped to the snow-covered grass, seemingly unconscious.

The possessed youth then turned back to the matter at hand.

"Now, where did we leave off, Linda? I think it was the part where you're going to answer for leaving me to get taken by—"

The near-revelatory spiel was unfortunately cut off when both were distracted by the terror-stricken screams of a young boy around the age of eight as he suddenly turned the corner.

"Help me! Please! The monster killed my mom! It's after me!"

"The energies of terror that boy is giving off," Lem's voice said. "I need to feed on it. But I can't do that in this body."

"Carol Anne, no--!"

Lem tumbled to the ground as the incorporeal etheric form of Carol Anne Nellis voluntarily stepped out of his body. Her alabaster white form with completely black eyes turned to the screaming young boy. She raised her arms and smiled as she drank in the terror he was experiencing based on the ill-fated encounter he and his now deceased mother had with the rakshasa during the past hour.

*I don't even gotta hit this one with the scream. Whatever he went through recently was more than enough to set this off. Oh, how delicious these emotions are!*

Linda ran over to Lem and lifted him up. Much to her relief, the shaken young boy's eyes were back to normal. But all his anguish had returned.

"My sister, Cecelia! That asshole killed her! Right in front of me!"

"Lem, I'm so sorry," Linda replied, trying her best to comfort the grief-stricken youth. "For what it's worth, though, when Carol Anne possessed you, she threw him up against that wall over there. He's done for."

"Who the hell is Carol Anne? Is she the one who... took me over?"

"You remember what happened when you were possessed?"

"Kinda, partly. Is she... some sorta ghost?"

"Yes. She was my best friend when we were children. But... look, it's a long story. She's dead now, and she's very confused and... honestly, really dangerous. I gotta find a way to reason with her. But she did fix your leg."

"She did?" Lem stood up and noticed how far reduced both the pain and the size of the bullet wound was. "Shit, she did! I gotta find my brother Jake now!"

"Lem... that killer in the Santa suit murdered him. He said so when he attacked us a few minutes ago."

"No!" Lem sunk his face into his hands. "I thought I remembered hearing him... say that when that ghost had control of me. But... it can't be true."

"I... think it is, Lem. I'm so sorry." She embraced the crying boy, doing her best to comfort him.

"And... I think I recognized the killer from reports I saw on TV. And from pictures in magazines collected by my friends, who are obsessed with true crime shit. I think he was Virgil Kennedy. One of the worst serial killers ever. You're lucky to be alive right now, Lem. Don't throw that away."

Linda gave the crying boy another quick consoling hug before grabbing his shoulders and making him look at her.

"Listen, Lem! I need you to be a hero, like your brother was. Carol Anne is threatening that little boy, and we have to stop her."

"H-how?"

"We can't attack her physically when she's not inside someone's body. But if we let her take over someone and *then* attack, we'd risk hurting or killing the person she possessed. But that coin may be key to stopping her."

"The coin? Is it…?"

"Yes, it's the one you picked up that released her in the first place. She was killed by something or someone while she was holding it and became linked to it somehow. We can trap her in it. But she can make it move around when she isn't trapped inside it unless someone is holding it. Still, it's dangerous for someone to hold it, because she can take possession of that person very quickly, or use it to open up warp portals, or something like that."

"I think I dropped the coin when I fell."

"Let's look for it, before she's done with that boy and moves it—"

"Linda? Is that you, hun?"

Linda turned towards the familiar voice to see none other than her grief counselor standing at the corner. Mable was the only person who seemed to understand her pain over losing Carol Anne, the guilt she experienced… and that earned her trust. But what was she doing here?

"Mable?"

"Yes, it's me," Mable said with her usual friendly smile. "Come over here and I'll help you out."

"Lem, come here! We have to get out of here!"

"Jake?" Lem said as he clearly saw his brother standing at the corner, not Mable.

"Yes, little bro, it's me."

"I thought you was dead?"

"No, I would never let that asshole kill me. I'm right here, and I'm waiting to take you home."

That was when the hysterical little boy that the ghostly Carol Anne was feeding off came to his senses. Seeing the two people confused over the presence of a person they trusted that could not possibly be present there, and the fact that both saw a different person, knocked him out of his crying stupor. He forced himself to ignore the terrifying apparition of a girl with black eyes standing before him and literally feeding off his misery to shout a warning.

"No! Don't listen to whoever you think you're seein'! It's a monster! A monster that eats people! It can make itself look like someone you know and trust! It killed my mother!"

Linda and Lem wanted to listen… but not nearly as much as they wanted to believe what they were seeing. After what they had both been through, they needed the comfort provided by these people, along with their offers to take them away from this nightmare. They began walking towards the visions they respectively saw, and Mable/Jake smiled and eagerly extended her/his arms to embrace the two. The rakshasa would be eating quite well this night.

"No! Don't go near that thing!" the boy yelled as he tried to run over to them.

"No," said the hungry ghost that Carol Anne Nellis had tragically become. "You're lying. And I want more of your feelings of terror. I'll make you give me more!"

The ghostly girl moved her mouth into a hideous "O" shape and released a piercing scream that cut into the boy like a sonic lance. He fell to the ground as not only did his eardrums feel close to bursting, but his mind was suddenly filled with amplified images of his deepest, most nightmarish fears.

These included images of his mother being torn up and ravenously devoured by the monster that killed her less than an hour ago… only now he could actually *see* the attack occurring based upon the worst abuses of his imagination, rather than merely hearing it. He was also buffeted by imagery of grinning gang members tearing off his mother's clothes and molesting her in front of him while she screamed for help a little boy could not provide; and a huge centipede attacking and devouring his pet terrier Punk that they had to put down last year.

Needless to say, Lyle Goldberg was on the ground screaming, crying, flailing, and begging the ghost girl to stop. But all the former Carol Anne

Nellis could think of was the luscious energy food he was providing for her. All vestiges of the kindly, thoughtful little girl she had been appeared to have been wiped away when she was killed and became what she now was.

As for Linda and Lem, they continued walking towards their doom… when an unexpected factor suddenly entered the fray. Virgil Thorne had awakened and shrugged off the impact of getting hurled against the wall by the possessed boy. He recovered his bat and observed his two targets walking towards some individual who was concealed in the shadows at the corner.

*I don't know how the kid had gotten so strong, or how he's walking straight after I blew a hole the size of a golf ball in his fucking leg. But it don't matter! Whoever they're walking towards must have offered them help. It would serve them right if it turned out to be a pimp or someone from the organ-selling black market. But whoever that fuckwad is, he's not taking* my *kills!*

Virgil raised his bat and within the moment a rampaging Killer Santa rushed towards a short cut behind the parking lot he had used before.

As the entranced Linda and Lem approached the glamour-inducing rakshasa, the demon raised its huge taloned hands and prepared to pounce. Instead, it was staggered when Virgil stepped out of the shadows behind it and slammed it in the back with his Louisville slugger. The impact, painful even to the bulky, supernaturally enhanced monstrosity, caused it to lose the concentration required to utilize its power to telepathically pluck images from the minds of its targets.

Linda and Lem were startled as the spell of glamour was suddenly broken and saw the rakshasa revealed for the hideous being it truly was.

"Shit!" Lem exclaimed. "That kid was right! It's a monster that disguises itself. Jake isn't alive!"

"Lem, you need to stay strong!" Linda stated firmly. "We need to go rescue the boy while that monster and Kennedy distract each other!"

The rakshasa turned towards its unexpected attacker and howled at him, baring its two tusk-like upper teeth. It would be taking a different meal now.

"Oh fuck!" Virgil hollered as he saw the beast standing before him. "I don't know what in fuck's name you are, but I can see it's either you or me. Put your money on me, motherfucker!"

The demon lunged at the mortal who dared attack it, and to its surprise, Virgil was swift enough to batter it back with two quick blows to the head with his bat. But the rakshasa was supernaturally resilient with healing abilities to match, so taking it down for the count would be no easy task. The otherworldly beast shrugged off the hits and attacked again with a roar of fury.

"You don't go down easy, do you?"

Virgil raised the bat and swung it at the monster again, only this time it blocked the attack with its muscular arm. The demon then swung its enormous hand, whose strength and razor-like talons cleaved the hardwood bludgeon in half.

"Shit! Well, I got more tricks up my sleeve, bitch!"

Virgil swiftly brandished the kitchen knife he had hidden in one of his Santa coat pockets. With a frenzied scream, the serial killer rushed forward slashing and stabbing. He inflicted several bloody wounds on the demon's face, arms, and torso, thus proving that its skin was more vulnerable to cold steel than lead bullets, the latter of which had little effect.

Nevertheless, the monster still healed at an accelerated rate, and it was exceedingly difficult to slay without a crossbow that was specially blessed by a Hindu brahman. And Virgil knew nothing of that, nor even exactly what he was up against. He simply had a psychotic resistance to fear and would attack anything that stood in his way.

*This thing is* strong, *and it can take a load of punishment. I gotta go for the eyes!*

Virgil raised his knife and took the stabbing shot he had planned. Much to the demon's further surprise, he evaded its swinging claw and managed to plunge the blade an inch into its right eye before pulling it out again. The man-eating monstrosity was still not delivered a lethal blow, but the injury inflicted in such a sensitive organ by cold steel was quite painful and would take a while to heal up properly. The demon staggered back, roaring in pain and rage while covering its perforated red eye.

*I did it! Now, if I can just get it in the throat…*

Virgil went for that universal vulnerability and the knife in his grip sailed through the air towards the beast's thick neck with impressive speed for a mere human. This time, however, the rakshasa focused its vision through its one good eye and swung its left hand at its assailant. Its claws tore through the scarlet lining of Virgil's Santa uniform and sent him flying through the air. He landed in the darkness of the parking lot with a loud thud. The demon observed the blood dripping down its nails and surmised that this mortal with supreme temerity would soon bleed out.

In the meantime, the rakshasa would pursue the other group of mortals that it had previously targeted. The time taken for the hunt would give its wounded eye a chance to fully heal.

\*\*\*

Linda and Lem both rushed to Lyle's aid, who was still in the process of being besieged by Carol Anne's spirit scream.

"I think I know where I dropped the coin," Lem noted. "But if I pick it up she can take me over again, right?"

"I have an idea," Linda shared. "Use your glove to pick it up. Don't let it touch your skin. I'm thinking she can't possess you unless the metal is in contact with your skin."

"But how do I suck her into the coin and trap her in it, or whatever?"

"I think – yes, threaten to throw it far away. I think if it gets too far from her, and she doesn't move it herself, she will get sucked into it and trapped. Then I can keep her from hurting others until I find a way to help her."

"Why the fuck you gotta help her for, Linda? She's some kinda monster."

"She was my friend! She still is. But she thinks I let her down and I have to show her that I didn't."

As the two ran down the rancid streets of Detroit's East Side on this very non-festive Christmas Eve, Linda and Lem saw the hungry ghost that was once a sweet little girl named Carol Anne Nellis standing in the middle of the road, her etheric attire resembling tatterdemalion versions of the late '60s clothing she had on the night she vanished and died. The whipping chill winds had no effect on her, nor did the blowing snow seem to bother

her coal black eyes. She stood there looking both terrifying and strangely beautiful, a vision of white in a season associated with that color.

Several feet away from her, laying on his back in the snow-shrouded asphalt, was the small form of Lyle Goldberg. Though she had already drained the bulk of his emotional energy and was no longer bombarding him with her combo of sonic and psychic attack, he still served as a wondrous reserve of fuel should she require it. The boy was still sniffling but was now too exhausted and in shock from the brutal assault on his psyche to make much of a struggle.

"There she is," Linda whispered to Lem. "Find that coin."

"Don't worry, I know where I dropped it," he whispered back. "I wouldn't be doing this with you if I didn't. I don't want that bitch screaming at me or possessing me again."

As the two finally approached within earshot of the girl spectre on these mostly deserted streets, Linda did what she could to distract her no longer living friend from Lem's purpose.

"Hi, Carol Anne. Can we please talk?"

"Hi, Linda. Did you come looking for me so you can face your punishment?"

"No. I came to talk. And to do something that's for your own good."

"Linda! I got the coin in my glove!" Lem suddenly shouted.

"No!" the ghostly girl wailed like the banshee she was now related to. "Give it here!"

"No!" Lem countered. "I'll throw it far. Really far. You'll get trapped in it again!"

"You were in on this, Linda! You were a traitor to me again!" the ghost decreed.

"Carol Anne, I swear on my life I don't know what happened to you!" Linda repeated. "I wasn't a traitor then, and I'm not one now. But you're hurting people, like that little boy there. He already lost his mother to a monster tonight. The person you used to be would never have done anything like this. If your older self were here, she would be helping us stop you."

"Hee! Hee! My older self died when I was taken, Linda. Now I've become… this. All because you didn't save me."

"Stop with the guilt bullshit! I would have helped you if I saw what had happened to you!"

"Tell the black kid to give me the coin or I'll start projecting terror into the white kid again."

"No! We won't let you!" Linda screamed.

"I'll throw this fucking thing as far as I can!" Lem shouted. "I'll drop it down that underground vent over there! Then you're ass will get trapped down in the sewers and no one will ever be able to get you out and help you!"

"Lem! Don't do that!" Linda pleaded.

"Well, what the fuck then? I'm not gonna let that bitch torture the boy no more!" Lem decreed.

"She's my friend! I can't fail her again!"

"Whatever she used to be, that thing ain't your friend no more!"

The moment was decided when Lyle suddenly turned his head, and in a weak voice said, "The... monster... that killed my mom. Look out. It's... coming."

Linda and Lem turned around to see the rakshasa approaching them sans any attempt at a disguise. It was concerned that the same illusion may not work on those two again, and it was more than pleased to kill them with full knowledge of what was coming. Visible in its full hideous glory, the fanged monstrosity with a head of long bushy hair roared at them in anger as well as cursing them in an ancient language they did not understand.

"Shit!" Lem said. "That other thing is coming again!"

"Then the white boy didn't lie!" Carol Anne yelled. "I won't let it kill you when I still have business with you!"

The girl spectre stepped forward and bombarded the Hindu demon with her spirit scream. The creature bellowed in agony and fell to its tree-stump-like knees as its large pointy ears felt as if they were being torn from its skull. Worse than that were the stream of magnified images of Brahma slowly burning it to ashes; and a horde of gigantic Hindu *pujari* descended on it with specially blessed crossbows that perforated it over every square inch of its grotesque body.

The rakshasa, however, was not without formidable psychic resources of its own. The creature concentrated on blocking the wave of sound so as to grab an image from the ghost girl's mind. That was nothing less than a projection of Linda.

"Don't hurt me, Carol Anne. We're still friends!" said the rakshasa's mental projection of Linda Laughton.

"Linda…?" was the ghost's response, as the psychic resonance of the demon's glamour made her *want* to believe in her friend's continued loyalty this time.

"No! It's not her!"

Able to look past the rakshasa's illusion due to her own formidable psychic faculties, the hungry ghost doubled down on her scream attack… which caused the rakshasa to do the same with its own mental assault.

Linda and Lem took this battle as an opportunity to run to the little boy and see to him.

The older girl turned him over to see the boy shivering from a combination of the cold and a severe anxiety attack.

"It's going to be okay!" the older girl said to him. "I'm Linda. This here is Lem. We're here to help you."

"I'm… Lyle. That big hairy demon killed my mother…"

"I know," Linda replied gently. "And we'll find a way to stop it, I promise. Lem lost his brother and sister to that killer in the Santa suit around the same time you lost your mom. So, he understands. And… I lost my best friend ten years ago, and she became the monster that just hurt you."

Linda had to struggle again not to burst into tears at the thought of all the death and trauma surrounding her.

The stalemate between the rakshasa and the hungry ghost was broken by a by now familiar, and in its own way, equally deadly source.

The three young humans, along with the demon and the ghost, turned as they heard the loud screeching tires and a revving motor behind them. This turned out to be the police squad car pilfered from Officer Jack Burns by Virgil Kennedy after murdering him earlier that night. In fact, the lawman's dead and rictus-stiffened body was still beside the Santa-garbed psychopath in the passenger seat as the Killer Santa sped towards the section of the street where the demon and the ghost girl were fighting.

"Here comes Santa Claus, here comes Santa Claus… driving like a maniac down the lane!" Virgil cynically sang as he aimed the speeding vehicle directly towards the rakshasa.

He slammed into the Hindu demon and dragged it through the street until the serial killer veered the car so it smashed the long-haired beast up against the side of the tenement. The creature was stunned but still alive and visibly enraged, pounding deep dents into the vehicle's solid steel trunk with its massive fists.

"Shit! What does it take to kill you, bitch?" Virgil griped.

The Killer Santa quickly put the car in reverse, backed it up, pushed the gear selector stick back into the drive position, and then slammed his foot on the accelerator. The car went forward and again crushed the rakshasa between the severely dented front end of the squad car and the exterior brick wall of the building. Blood trickled from the demon's mouth as Virgil cackled like the madman he actually was.

Nevertheless, after a few moments of standing mostly still, the rakshasa began healing even from these terrible injuries. The demon made this fact known by suddenly emitting enraged growls and pounding furiously on the hood of the car, gradually smashing the steel surface into scrap metal.

"Uh oh," Virgil murmured to himself. "This Christmas Eve is now starting to suck big gray rhinoceros balls."

Within moments, the front of the police vehicle was pummeled into scrap metal. Virgil frantically rifled through the pockets of Officer Burns' corpse searching for any possible weapon that might better his odds of surviving the rakshasa's coming onslaught.

"Shit! There's nothing in this pig's pants except for his dick! Wait a minute, here's something…"

The killer was disappointed that what he pulled from Burns' pocket was nothing more than a spray bottle of mace. Virgil realized that it might be effective if sprayed directly into the demon's still injured left eye.

Before he could get the chance to test it out, however, the Santa-clad maniac found himself yelling in horror and surprise as the rakshasa flipped the demolished squad car up and over. It landed upside down on its roof with a devastating smash. Nothing seemed to be stirring within, and the demon turned to begin approaching its three other targets once more.

Just then, some new players *finally* entered the scene. The sirens and spinning cherry lights of two approaching squad cars rushed onto the vicinity and screeched to a halt. Eight officers quickly disembarked between the twin vehicles. Linda ran up to them, with the two boys following closely behind.

"Hold it right there!" the lead cop said, pointing his revolver at her. "Don't make another move!"

"Don't shoot, Officer!" Linda appealed. "I'm not a criminal and those two are just kids! We need help!"

The hardened Detroit cop was not taking any chances, however. "You heard me! Don't move and put your hands on your head!"

Linda quickly complied, with the boys following suite, but the cop's action riled Carol Anne.

The phantom girl turned to face the cop and said, "No! She's mine to punish!"

"What... the... fuck...?" the cop standing next to the first said. "Bob, look at that girl... if that's what she is. Is she sick or something?"

"I said... get away from Linda with that gun," the spectral girl demanded.

"Shut up, girl!"

"I warned you. Experience terror."

With that, Carol Anne unleashed her spirit scream on the lead cop. Within a second he dropped his piece and lay on the slush-filled street screaming in horror as his mind was filled with larger than life images of two gangbangers forcing his mouth open while a third poured a cup of spiders down his gullet; a fourth gang member began castrating him with a large gleaming razor blade; and a distorted image of his father, who had committed suicide years ago, shooting himself through his left ear over and over again, as if it was a news clip stuck on repeat.

Realizing what was happening even if his mind failed to understand it, the cop next to the first opened fire on the ghost, but his bullets simply passed through her to no effect.

"What the hell...?"

Christofer Nigro
*The Yuletide Massacre Melee*
Yuletide Horrors Volume 1

Before he could react any further, the law officer was suddenly seized by the huge claws of the rakshasa, whom he failed to see approach. The demon bit a chunk out of his throat and then ravenously began to devour him from the neck on down.

"Oh my god!" Linda shouted while the boys screamed in horror.

"Let's get the hell outta here!" Lem bellowed, and his two new friends followed fast on his heels.

A third officer fired several shots at the beast rapidly devouring his fellow lawman, but to no more discernible effect than the first salvo of bullets had on the phantom girl. The cop then unsheathed his billy club and attacked the rakshasa with it, while two of the other officers brandished their own batons and followed suit. That turned out to be an epic mistake.

Despite the beat down delivered on the demon by all three cops, the creature withstood and disemboweled two of them with a sudden slashing motion in opposite directions by both claws simultaneously. The final cop in this particular melee fell to his knees in trembling terror as he watched the bowels of his two eviscerated partners spill out onto the snow-covered street before they slumped over on their own guts. All he could do is scream like hell as the rakshasa leapt on him and rapidly stripped his bones of almost every inch of flesh.

At the same time, the four cops from the second vehicle had run over to the toppled squad car they were certain belonged to Officer Jack Burns, whom they had strangely lost contact with hours earlier. They were surprised to see a black boot kick out one of the already broken windows on the driver's side. Seconds later, the upper portion of a man dressed like none other than Santa Claus himself slid out. His face and neck were covered with cuts and bruises, and the front of his distinctive red coat was torn open to reveal a nasty shoulder wound beneath the cloth that looked as if he had been raked by a grizzly. All four authority figures glanced at each other with a perplexed expression.

"Little help here, officers?"

Two of the lawmen ran to help extricate the apparent helper of Santa out and to his feet.

"Thank you, kind sirs," said a grateful-sounding Virgil Kennedy, whom they failed to recognize under the fake beard.

For a moment, that is. "Hey, aren't you…?"

The cop was abruptly cut off when Virgil sprayed him in the eyes with mace. He then sliced open the the man's throat with a swift slash of his blade.

"Shhhhh…" he said in a Santa-esque fashion with his index finger over his pursed lips.

As this first cop fell, Virgil took the second by surprise by slicing his wrist just as he drew his revolver. The officer opened his mouth to yell in agony as he dropped the piece while simultaneously squeezing his slit wrist in a desperate attempt to staunch the blood loss. Before he could do so, Virgil sprayed what must have been half the bottle of mace in the man's mouth, nose, and eyes, causing his attempted scream of agony to be cut off as he began gagging. The serial killer then kicked him in the chin as hard as he could with his steel-toed boot, sending the cop onto his back, knowing he would bleed out within minutes.

The other two, who were checking the rest of the toppled vehicle to search for signs of Officer Burns, looked up at the commotion to see Virgil Kennedy wielding a billy club and a menacing grin.

"Don't worry about Officer Burns getting roughed up when the car was flipped, like I did. I can assure you he's been dead for hours. See, he's already stiffening like an earthworm under a hot summer's sun… wasn't bothered by it at all!"

"Jesus Christ it's Kennedy!" the third cop hollered.

"Heh! It's always an honor to be recognized."

Before the two remaining officers could go for their revolvers, Virgil smashed them across the foreheads with a single swing of his pilfered baton. He then quickly turned the nightstick against the one closest to him and literally battered his brains out.

The remaining cop crouched against the side of the inverted car and utilized his training for quick drawing his revolver to good effect. However, Virgil swiftly smacked the piece out of his hand with another swing of the billy club, cracking the officer's ulna at the same time.

The disarmed lawman yelped in pain and looked up in horror as he saw a grinning Santa standing above him with a raised baton.

"Guess who made my naughty list this year, pig?"

The officer barely had time to even consider begging for his life before Virgil took the matter out of his hands by smashing him into permanent retirement from life.

\*\*\*

"Run!" Lem bellowed as took off around the corner with Linda and Lyle following on his heels.

The trio ran past the first officer, who still lay on the street writhing in his extremities and screaming himself hoarse as the horrific visions projected into his psyche by Carol Anne continued to have effect. The girl apparition remained standing near him and drinking deeply of the emotional energy he emitted as his worst fears assaulted him with relentless abandon.

*I wish I could do something for that poor man,* Linda thought to herself. *But I must get these boys away from that demon and Kennedy. Then I have to find a way to help Carol Anne even if it does kill me. She would've done the same for me before she became this… thing.*

The fleeing threesome took off around the corner and into a nearby alley. Their hope was to find a short cut out of there, possibly even a way to the subway system so they could leave the vicinity and find help. What they found instead was a dead-end.

"Oh, shit, no!" Lem muttered.

"No…" Lyle murmured in a tone of despair.

The three turned around as they heard a growling sound. Standing in front of them blocking their way out of the alley was the massive figure of the rakshasa. The demon snarled, baring its deadly teeth and raising its razor-sharp claws as it moved in for the triple kill.

Just as suddenly, Lyle lost all sense of fear as the emotion was replaced by something different but every bit as strong.

"You killed my mother, you bastard ass!" the little boy yelled as he raised his fists. "Now I'm gonna kill you!"

"Lyle, no!" Linda yelled as she grabbed the small boy and held him with all her might.

69

But why did she? The three of them were demon food in a few moments anyway. So, why not allow the boy the dignity of dying while fighting for his life and attempting to avenge his mom?

"Linda… I got no choice," Lem lamented as he took his glove out of his coat pocket and dropped the coin in his hand.

"Lem, no…"

"I gotta let her take me over again. It's the only way I'll have a chance of killing that fuckhead and gettin' us outta this. Your ghost and the demon will only stalemate each other going back and forth with the mental whammy thing. This is the only way."

Tears began flowing down the girl's face as she held Lyle in place. She knew Lem was correct.

"Carol Anne!" she shouted. "Get your ass over here, unless you want this monster to kill me before you get your chance!"

Within a second the girl spectre was hovering inches off the ground in front of the alley.

Lem held up the coin in his fingers as the advancing rakshasa was now just a few feet away from ripping into his prey.

"Come take me over, ghost girl! Hurry!"

Since he held the coin, Carol Anne was able to swoop towards him at blurring speed. Her incorporeal form passed clear through the rakshasa and entered Lem's body, causing his eyes to go dark and the coin to stick to his hand with a slight glow as she took control.

The rakshasa singled out Linda and swung his huge claw at her throat… only to find it stopped in mid-swipe by Lem's now superhuman grip.

"You don't get to kill my friend!" Carol Anne screamed through Lem's mouth as she directed him to deliver a punch to the beast's stomach followed by a haymaker to its jaw that sent it staggering.

She then directed Lem's body to stand its ground and raise his "dukes" for the next round. The youth was quite tall for ten years of age, pushing '5'7" so he hardly looked like a small child but resembled a legitimate pugilist ready to rumble.

"C'mon, Lyle!" Linda yelled as she pulled by the boy by the lapel of his winter coat and directed him to flee the alley.

Realizing what had occurred, the rakshasa rushed forward and pushed the possessed Lem against the wall, cracking the front layer of brick behind it with the force. The possessed and enhanced youth, under Carol Anne's direction, grabbed the demon by the throat and squeezed with maximum pressure. The creature began choking but broke the hold by once again slamming the boy up against the wall. It then slashed him across the left side of his face, ripping a portion of the skin off.

Carol Anne felt that and yelped in pain. She knew that she had to make her host fight much harder if she hoped for him to avoid being injured badly enough that her ghostly form was forced out of his body… in which case the beast would tear Lem to pieces in seconds and resume stalking Linda.

The monster took another swipe towards Lem's face, but he was quick and strong enough to catch its wrist, struggling with all his enhanced might to keep its claws from progressing further towards his flesh. The beast then moved to sink its teeth into his throat, but the possessing ghost directed her host to grasp the monster's throat with his other hand to halt that as well, thus resulting in a second concurrent struggle between the two.

Then the rakshasa grabbed the boy's entire head in its other hand and slammed it against the brick wall, pushing it over half an inch into the stonework. The ghost girl's host body continued to hold fast under her control despite being stunned by that last move… but for how long? She knew she had to kill this thing ASAP, but she wasn't certain if she could manage that before the demon killed her host body first.

As Linda and Lyle ran outside the alley, they were suddenly confronted by a grinning Virgil Kennedy, who had a knife in one hand a police baton in the other. He was still on his feet despite having his right shoulder torn open by the rakshasa and having received numerous other beatings and abrasions, including a right eye that was almost swollen shut.

"Well, well… fancy meeting you two again. I hope you weren't thinking of leaving before we had ourselves a little Christmas torture party."

Lyle suddenly darted to his left and attempted to flee.

"Oh, no you don't, you little prick!" Virgil shouted as he used his remarkable speed to halt the boy's escape attempt by grabbing the hood of his coat and choking him.

As the killer raised the knife to slice the boy across the back of his neck Linda leapt on the psycho's back and bit into the side of his face as hard as she could. Virgil shouted in pain before shoving his elbow back into the girl's stomach, dislodging her teeth from his cheek and causing her to go skidding on her back over the ice.

"You stupid cunt!" the Killer Santa yelled as blood streamed out of the bite mark she made on his face. He then raised his knife. "And speaking of 'cunt,' I'm gonna shove this in there and gut you upwards like a fucking fish!"

This statement was heard by Carol Anne as she continued grappling with the rakshasa in Lem's body.

"No! You won't kill Linda!"

With a surge of emotion-fueled energy, the ghost directly her host to use all his enhanced might to throw the demon off him. The hurled demon smashed into the section of the building that formed the right side of the alley, practically crashing clear through the brickwork. She then directed Lem's body to run towards the Killer Santa at top speed.

Just as Virgil grabbed Linda by her long brown hair and raised the knife to plunge it into her nether regions Lem's hand grabbed him by the back of his scarlet coat and tossed him to the other side of the alley with ease. He bounced off the far wall and landed on a snowbank.

"Carol Anne… Lem's face. He's really hurt. Can you…?"

"Yea, I have to fix this. Gimme a minute."

Lem's body stood taut as Carol Anne poured a substantial proportion of the emotional energy she had absorbed from the police officer into her host's cellular structure. As a result, the severe tears on his face began growing new flesh and skin right in front of Linda and Lyle's very eyes as well as healing the concussion on the back of his skull. Within moments, the torn face was nothing more than a long, thin, barely bleeding cut.

"Nice trick," came Virgil's voice as the ever-resilient serial killer forced himself back to his feet and raised his knife. "But it won't save you. Now we're gonna play autopsy, and I'm gonna be the coroner!"

"Come and get me," Carol Anne said through Lem's larynx, "so I can break you in two."

That contest was thwarted before it began, however, when the rakshasa hurled a huge chunk of ice at Lem. The giant shard of heavily packed snow struck him between his shoulder blades. The object was too blunt to cause any severe damage to his enhanced form, but the impact was sufficient to knock him off his feet and cause Carol Anne's ghostly essence to be forced out of his body. Her ectoplasmic form rolled across the ice as if it had no weight whatsoever (which it technically didn't) and kept doing so for over a hundred yards distant.

Linda and Lyle ran to the now back-to-normal Lem, helping the tall boy to his feet.

"Ugh… my back…" he said as he stood up, grateful that he was able to walk.

"I don't think anything's broken," Linda said, "but Carol Anne was knocked out of you."

*"Now* let's see you kill me, boy!" the serial killer taunted while again raising his blade. "Let's see how bad ass you are without that fucking ghost inside you."

Lem stood his ground and put up his "dukes" again. "You killed my sister and my brother for no reason at all. I don't need the ghost. I'll *still* kick your ass!"

"Oh ho, nice bravado, kid. It's gonna be fun cutting you to pieces."

That contest was likewise destined to be denied, however, as the rakshasa's snarl caused the quartet to turn around. The beast swiftly exited the alley and headed for Linda's group, having mostly healed from the broken shoulder blade inflicted on it by the enhanced Lem.

"Fucking *you* again!" Virgil exclaimed.

The rakshasa moved its attention from its three chosen targets to the one mortal who continually attempted to kill it, while at the same time evading the beast's several counter efforts to do the same to him in turn. The demon roared angrily at the serial killer.

"All right, let's finish this!" Virgil shouted while raising his knife into a defensive posture. "You think you can do me? *C'mon then!"*

The Hindu monstrosity roared in obvious acceptance to the challenge, raising its talons and baring its fangs as it moved to put paid to this annoying mortal adversary once and for all.

Linda maneuvered Lem and Lyle into taking advantage of this to flee… only to find their path blocked by the hovering spectral form of Carol Anne.

"Trying to run out on me again, Linda?"

The ghostly lass then waved one of her hands to send the coin off to a location out of the trio's field of vision so they could no longer use it against her.

"Now I'm gonna use the time those two are distracted trying to kill each other to deal with you."

"Please listen to me, Carol Anne…"

"No! I won't let you betray me again, Linda. You and your little friends are gonna experience terror like you never knew to be possible."

\*\*\*

Before anything further could occur on either front, however, all present at the scene, human and otherwise, were distracted by a warm light that emanated from within a nearby bus stop enclosure. Out of it emerged a rotund but robust looking older man dressed in red and green with a bristling white beard, black gloves & boots, and rosy, red cheeks. The swirling snow began surrounding him and whirling around his form as if recognizing him as this natural force's master.

The handsome-grandfatherly figure stepped out of the enclosure and made a statement with firm authority behind it. "Okay, there shall be no more of this. All of you who represent chaos and evil will cease and desist… or face the wrath of my light, with all the might of winter reinforcing it."

"Linda," Lyle whispered, "is it… really *him* this time?"

"Yes," she replied, with tears trickling down her cheeks. "It is. Somehow I just *know* it is."

"Holy shit," Lem stated.

"Language, young man," the cheery but godly figure said while raising an index finger.

"Sorry, man."

"You have gotta be kidding me…" Virgil said as he turned to face the imposing figure.

"I assure you there is nothing false about me, Mr. Kennedy. Unlike the falsehood you propagated this night. How dare you use my image to commit such horrific acts against your fellow man. How dare you despoil what I represent. What this very *day* represents. Suffice to say, you have made my naughty list."

"You know, fuck all of this!" the killer exclaimed as he raised his blade and brought it down on the portly figure.

"Really now, Mr. Kennedy," the gentleman said as he raised a finger. "Must you force me to embarrass you as I give you further proof of the authenticity you sorely lack?"

Before Virgil's blade could strike its target, the knife froze solid in mid-strike. The figure then snapped his fingers and the frozen metal shattered.

"Oh, fuck…" the killer lamented as he looked at the handle of the knife now bereft of its blade.

"And that language of yours… that just won't do at all."

He snapped his fingers and Virgil's lips froze shut. Try as he might, the killer was unable to pull the ice off his mouth.

"Now, let us talk penance. Unlike you, I do not kill. I *will* not kill, because that is not what I am about. But there are… darker sides to the force that empowers me that does allow me to enact appropriate punishments. And since I believe it is more likely than not that you are beyond redemption, Mr. Kennedy, I must remove you from human contact until, when, or if the opportunity may arise that you can prove useful to the forces of good."

He snapped his fingers again and Virgil Kennedy was engulfed by a whirling dervish of snow that revealed he had been transported far away once it ceased spinning and dissipated.

"Where… did you send him?" Linda asked.

"Where he will do the most good for now, serving as a monument to his folly."

The rakshasa growled at the strange interloper, knowing who he was and familiar with the force of the cosmos he represented… and the demon did not want to risk attacking him.

"As for you, demon. You have killed and desecrated enough innocent mortals with that horrific appetite of yours. It is time you ceased being the force for death and conquest that your race represents and be the one among them to serve the greater good."

The creature growled again and could be heard muttering a single coherent word. "Nooo…"

"My dear beast, you simply have no choice in the matter. Your penance has begun as conscription into my services."

The figure raised his hand and shimmering chains suddenly appeared around the rakshasa, enclosing his neck and arms. The demon struggled ferociously, but the bonds would not break.

"Do not waste your efforts, as strong as you may be. Not even the Krampus could break those chains. And they once even held Mr. Scratch himself for a time."

The figure then turned towards the still-hovering spectre of Carol Anne. His visage betrayed a look of sorrow and sympathy rather than anger.

"And you, my poor dear… you found yourself pushed down this dark, thorny path by no fault of your own. Perhaps you will believe me when I tell you that your friend was not to blame, and she would have given her all to save you if she had but witnessed the dreadful fate you wandered into."

"No… nooooo!" the hungry ghost shouted. "She… is a traitor!"

"She is not. In time, you will come to accept that. But alas, for now, you cannot be allowed to harm others while in this state."

"No! You weren't there to save me either! Like you just saved those three! I won't believe you! And I won't let you capture meeeee…"

As she uttered those words, the ghost summoned the full power of the coin, now under her control, and transported herself far away before even the godly figure of Kris Kringle could act to prevent it.

"Oh dear, that one," he lamented.

"Can you… help her?" Linda asked.

"Yes," he replied. "But more importantly, I shall provide you with the assistance to find her and help her yourself. I know someone who is perfect for the task, and I give you my word she shall be contacting you within just a few days. You need do nothing but await her arrival wherever you may be."

"Thank you so much." Linda struggled to hold back tears yet again. "But… what about Lyle and Lem? They… lost everything."

"I am aware of their terrible losses, and I deeply regret not being able to get here sooner to personally deal with this triune threat to the city on this sacred evening. I shall compensate for that by inviting both young gentlemen to come and live with me in Christmas Village. There they will have ample support, and many opportunities to overcome their inner pain and become outstanding forces for good. Their heroic actions this night prove they have that potential and would make honored additions to my hallowed village."

"I'll… I'll go," Lem said, trying to hold back his tears. "I got no one now that Jake and Cecelia are… gone. I think going there with him will be lots better than any orphanage in this world."

"I'm… gonna go too," Lyle said, this time bereft of tears. "I don't have a mommy anymore, and I never had a daddy or anyone else. So, *you* can be my daddy. I'm not gonna cry no more; I'm gonna try to be a big boy."

"No shame in grieving over such a loss, little man," the figure said. "You have shown more than enough courage to offset the fears that started you on your previous path. Now, let us be off. The North Polar region awaits."

Just as Mr. Kringle turned to create the whirling portal that would see himself, Lem, and Lyle to his other-dimensional version of Earth's North Pole, with the captive rakshasa in tow, Linda decided she had another important question.

"Um, sir… may I please ask you just two more things?"

"You have certainly earned that much, young lady," Kringle said as he turned. "Please do ask."

"Well, first… did you imply earlier that it wasn't a coincidence that all three of those threats appeared here on Christmas Eve at the same time?"

"It was not. It was an event known to those in my circle as a *convergence.* They were all attracted here at nearly the exact same time, due to the energies produced by some of the… darker aspects of the Yule force. It was significant enough that it would come to my attention and merited my personal intervention rather than leaving it to one of my agents, or to more conventional forces to deal with."

"I… see. I think. Okay, now question number two. And please do not take this the wrong way, but… I sorta sympathize with how Carol Anne felt. Why does someone with your power allow terrible things to happen? Why didn't you save her from whatever happened to her like you saved some of us tonight? Why do you allow people like Kennedy to become such awful killers and get away with so much of what they do before you finally step in like you did tonight?

"Okay, I know those were actually several questions, but I think they all intersect."

"Ho! Ho! Ho! Worry not, my dear. I can and shall answer.

"Putting aside the fact that not even I, who can circumvent time and space itself, may be literally everywhere at once, those who truly represent the forces of light are not at liberty to remove choices from human beings. We can help them along, deal with certain individual cases directly due to various factors too complex to discuss right now, and deal with particularly big threats quite directly… but we cannot *force* individual humans to take the side of light. We likewise cannot literally prevent every single person on a world of billions from suffering and death, which may lead to a higher purpose in a realm beyond this one.

"The greatest expression of love and benevolence is to grant freedom of choice to those under your care. Otherwise, they cannot grow and reap the true rewards that come with reaching such a plateau on their own.

"Moreover, there are, as mentioned before, darker aspects to the force I represent that provide a proper place even for evil in this cosmos, and true goodness cannot come about if it has no opposite to conquer and contrast itself against. I belong to an organization dedicated to building a far better world for humanity, but we can only help so far. Humanity must ultimately and collectively build a superior world order through its own efforts. The

Age of Aquarius may be upon it, and Aquarians may abound, but only mortals may bring its potential to true fruition."

"Now… if I have not lost you with my spiel, or even if I have, I and my new companions must be off. May the Light bless you, Linda Laughton, and a Merry Christmas to you."

With that said, Kringle waved his gloved hand and the snow formed another, albeit wider, whirling dervish around him and his companions. It was accompanied by a brilliant flash of light, and after the snowy whirlwind appeared to implode upon serving its purpose, a god had departed in its wake.

Linda began her trip home, eagerly awaiting the arrival of one who would help her to finally bring much needed peace to the friend she lost but still had the opportunity to save.

## EPILOGUE

The place is far off Niflheim, a frozen world inhabited by cold-hearted entities. It has now gained a new inhabitant, who materialized there quite suddenly during the day of Yule. The new arrival appeared to be a mortal man trapped in ice that surrounded his body, preserved without dying but unable to move, extricate himself from that spot, or be removed by others. And there Virgil Kennedy stands through the ages, a frozen monument to the folly of the dark path and where it will ultimately bring those who worship evil's might.

## END

# NICE TRY

**Bonus story by Dustin Dreyling – featuring the Krampus!**
**Originally published as a free download on the Wild Hunt Press**
**Facebook group circa Christmas 2020.**

"Let me down, guys, please!" Joshua wailed.

Peter, David, and Colin just laughed at him. They never stopped what they were doing, which was stringing the poor little kid up like a Christmas decoration to the big white spruce tree in the large front yard of their foster residence. They had already taped multiple glow sticks they had stolen from Sam's Mart to his body. Now they were stringing him up to several of the highest branches that were heavy enough to support the bound and crying nine-year old's weight.

David started whistling "Jingle Bells," and Colin joined in. Peter just laughed as he tied the final knot that would suspend Merle and Artis Cross' youngest foster child from the prickly branches of their biggest tree. The two heads of the household were passed out drunk in their beds on the second floor of the old white farmhouse where they all resided.

This reoccurring habit of the poor parental figures enabled the three boys to pick on young Joshua regularly, their disdain for him stemming from an unknown place. They just hated him -- he did not know why, and neither did they, and that made it all the more horrible. Not saying anything more to the kid they tormented often, the trio of naughty pre-teens went back inside the house, leaving the freezing youth hanging from the tree by himself.

Joshua shivered uncontrollably within the branches of the spruce. The needles of the tree stung him in a multitude of places and soon his face was pockmarked with frozen spots of blood. Barely conscious as hypothermia loomed, he had one last dreamy thought before all went dark. This came to him as he stared out of the tree through the color that the many glowsticks duct taped to his body cast over the coniferous needles surrounding him. It was a strange and terrifying thought…

*There's a monster out there.*

As Joshua slipped into unconsciousness, a dark form stepped out of the winter night. The crunch of its hooves punching into the snow with each purposeful step threatened to make the poor boy pee his pants from fright. The horned nightmare that had locked onto poor Joshua grinned, its clenched choppers severe and wicked looking -- like a mouth made in Hell. A shoestring of drool trailed from its demonic face. Glowing red eyes with a disturbingly green pupil in the center were the most festive thing about the Christmas horror closing in on the freezing boy.

Sometime later, he became aware once more, but he seemed to be floating in a warm place. It was pitch black and undulating. His whole existence shifted and moved with each… *step* that something took. Joshua was not sure what that meant, but somewhere in his mind, he knew that was accurate.

*"Krampus,"* something growled in his ear.

A cry of fright escaped him and Joshua flailed about for what seemed like several minutes before giving up. Wherever he was, it was like trying to escape the confines of way too many blankets while underwater -- except for the fact that he could breathe just fine. In fact, he was coming back so quickly from the hypothermia now, it was almost miraculous. It was so *warm* in this place.

*Inside his bag, the one he shoves naughty children into.*

The phantom voice echoed in his mind, its origin unknown. Its pitch was very child-like. Before his mind could protest his complacency to danger, the soothing heat of the logic-defying place Joshua was trapped within lulled him back to sleep. There, he dreamt of merry Christmases that he had never experienced before.

The Krampus moved toward the house, the glowing festive eyes training themselves on the upstairs bedroom window of the faux parents. In a series of short, rapidly barked phrases, its breath seemed to come alive. Twisted black, red, and green smoke came spiraling out of its maw, rising up in the air before it seemed to splatter all over the second story windows like paint tossed from a can. The supernatural substance spread out to consume the windows, the triple-colored liquid miasma covering the portals quickly. A dull glow resonated from each coated opening, the sealing process complete.

Krampus grinned again, more drool dropping to the snow.

*Time to get to work.*

It walked up the steps to the house, ripping the screen door open with nary a sound before pushing forward into the Cross' domicile. Ducking to enter the smelly, unkempt residence, Krampus's nostrils flared at the human stench assaulting its senses. It longed to be able to include adults on its list of miscreants that were rejected by the big man himself. It would never go hungry or minion-less again. Alas, its jurisdiction was only naughty children.

Fortunately, there were a few in the basement, playing video games after leaving their foster brother dangling from a tree on Christmas Eve, not caring if he lived or died. That was the naughtiest type of child, and it could practically taste their sins against the kid who was already in the bag slung over its shoulder. Its stomach growled in anticipation of the fear it would consume very soon. Joshua's terror had ceased long ago, as good children never remained afraid for long. It was just how the magic satchel worked. He would be very scared later, at the end of the night when Krampus pulled him out of it.

The monster of Christmas approached the basement stairs, the doorless opening revealing the flickering glow of a television at the bottom, where hushed voices gathered, talking and laughing past their bedtimes. More drool spattered on the floor from another gleeful grin full of fiendish teeth. The first hoof gently lowered itself to the first step, mindful of the spot in the middle where it knew a creak would give it away; that sudden knowledge was another supernatural perk. It was good to be Saint Nick's ninja-like, demon counterpart.

Joshua slept inside the bag, dreaming of a Christmas morning without his foster brothers, or his terrible excuses for parents. A family he had never known gathered around a brightly lit Douglas Fir, looking at him expectantly with bright smiles on their faces. Feeling part of a family for the first time in his life, his heart soared as he ran to them, the dream having fully taken over his psyche.

\*\*\*

"Do you guys smell that?" David asked, pausing of *Grand Theft Auto: San Andreas*.

"Yeah, what the hell is that?" Peter asked while covering his nose.

"It smells like hairy animal ass at the zoo," Colin said, looking back over his shoulder. "What the f—"

A taloned hand clutched the middle adolescent's head like a vise, blood being drawn from where the keratin pierced his flesh. Colin gasped, a meek whimper catching in his throat, as Peter and David looked back at the source of his anguish. Before either could react, Krampus snagged David's head in its other claw, a meaty slapping sound signaling the collision of its palm with the boy's face. David's muffled protests quickly took on a crying quality as he struggled along with Colin in Krampus' grip.

Peter squeaked in fright as Krampus' dropped bag opened on its own, unseen hands seemingly holding it open. In the blink of an eye, the Christmas demon shoved both boys into the dark recesses of the mind-boggling rucksack. Neither got out more than a peep before they disappeared from Peter's sight. After the bag cinched up tight on its own, he looked up into the face of Krampus, who was leaning down to leer at him. More drool spilled over its dark lips. Peter's eyes found themselves looking at the curved horns adorning its head, then locked onto the maddening red eyes with their green centers, glowing hellishly at him.

The boy ran up the stairs, wishing there had been a door on the basement stairwell. He tore through the kitchen, his stockinged feet slapping on the linoleum. For once, Peter was not worried about waking the terrible people that posed to the world as his parents. He screamed after this realization, yelling and hollering for the two dead-to-the-world people sleeping upstairs in the magic cocoon that Krampus had spun for them, keeping them oblivious to the monster's presence and its actions.

Peter raced down the short hallway at the top and turned the corner. Their bedroom door was open at the end of the next hall, and hope blossomed in the naughty boy. *Almost there,* he thought, never considering what he expected them to be able to do against a demon so soon after being roused from a drunken slumber. If he *could* wake them, that is.

Peter reached the doorway, his mouth opening as he sucked in a lungful of air to scream at them again.

"Help me—"

Krampus' vile claw wrapped around his face from behind, yanking the last boy back into the hallway and shoving him into the waiting void of the mysterious satchel before the pre-teen knew what had hit him. Peter's world synched up with his naughty brothers, all three bullies kicking, screaming, and flailing in the suffocating folds of the deceptive cloth haversack, never reaching or waking Joshua. Their panicked imaginations ran wild with predicting their dark futures.

The horned thing walked casually out of the Cross residence, a spring in its step as it went to leave with its prizes. It had been a good night so far, and it was only midnight. Krampus tried not to think about the youngest one, lest someone should hear its thoughts – like the Big Man himself. Suddenly, the smell of herd mammals filled its nose, the reindeer scent unmistakable. Krampus cursed itself for thinking about little Joshua too much.

"Where do you think you're going with young Joshua, Krampus?"

It spun around, knowing what it would see. On the roof of the aging farmhouse, sat a small herd of caribou, nine in total, all reined to an elaborate and exquisitely crafted silver, red, and gold sleigh. An impossibly large cloth bag that dwarfed Krampus' own sat in the back of the sled, overflowing with gravity-defying presents.

*Dammit,* Krampus thought. *I almost got away with it.*

Dustin Dreyling
*Nice Try*
Yuletide Horrors Volume 1

Krampus growled at Santa Claus, the red-suited fat man not looking so jolly while standing in front of the seasonal monster with his arms crossed and his mustached lips pursed in anger. The bearded man's red-pupiled green eyes blazed with fury at his helper's deviance. The Christmas demon put the bag full of children down, opening it for Santa. His superior sauntered over, his eyes locked with Krampus' as he reached into the bag. Distant cries from the three older foster brothers reached his ears. Santa's face crumpled in sadness for the briefest of seconds. Then he spoke into the blackness of Krampus' hellish holding cell for wayward children.

"I am very disappointed in you boys. You are mean to your little brother. I wish I could help you, but you are at the top of the naughty list -- you *left your brother outside to die!"*

Santa said the last part with anger in his voice, enough of it that even Krampus was unnerved by the ferocity. Then the big man reached into the bag and plucked out the sleeping Joshua. Cradling the boy in his arms, he returned to the sleigh on top of the house, leaping from the snowy ground up to the crowded roof like a superhero. He wrapped the boy in some red plush blankets he pulled from out of nowhere and nestled him next to the huge bag of yet undelivered toys in the backseat. Satisfied the child was secured and comfortable, he looked back at Krampus, a smirk on his jolly face.

"Nice, try," he said. "But good work all the same. I have a family in mind that deserves this little boy as much as he deserves them. Thank you for enabling me to give all of them a Merry Christmas!"

Santa Claus called out to each one of his antlered steeds to take to the sky, the flying deer-powered transport lifting off the roof and ascending into the night as it bent reality to its will. Laughing his trademark belly chuckle, Santa passed by Krampus, waving genuinely down at the demonic Christmas entity.

When he passed by, the horned thing flipped him off with one long, taloned middle finger. A final grin stretched across its lips before it lumbered off into the night, heading to visit the next horrible child on the naughty list while reminding itself to save some of its captures for minions this year.

Dustin Dreyling
*Nice Try*
Yuletide Horrors Volume 1

# END

# ABOUT THE AUTHORS

**Christofer Nigro** is a lifelong fan of the horror and sci-fi genres, along with comic books, superheroes, and pulp fiction. He has been running the soon-to-be-updated websites The Godzilla Saga and Warrenverse: The Amazing World of the Warren Comics Characters for years and years. He has had short stories published by Black Coat Press, Pro Se Press, Sirens Call Publications, Pulp Empire, Grinning Skull Press, Local Hero Press, and Horrified Press, with his first two novels published by Severed Press. He is the founder, owner, and editor-in-chief of Wild Hunt Press, which has a growing list of publications behind it, including the *Duel of the Monsters* anthology series and Christofer's *Nero* series of novels dealing with a certain angst-ridden teen werewolf, beginning with *Nero Book 1: The Beast Emerges.*

**Dustin Dreyling** is an avid fan of science fiction and horror, with a soft spot for all things kaiju. Originally hailing from White Bear Lake, Minnesota, he also likes proofreading novels, playing video games both old and new, and taking care of his planted freshwater aquariums. His first published story was featured in Zach Cole's linear horror anthology *The Experiment* published by Wild Hunt Press, and his short fiction can also be found in Wild Hunt's anthologies *Attack of the Kaiju Vol. 2: The Next Wave* and *Duel of the Monsters Vol. 1.* His first novel, the debut of his kaiju horror series *Primordial Soup: The First Batch,* was released in early 2020 from Wild Hunt Press.

Dustin is a lifelong native of Saint Paul, Minnesota, where he lives with the love of his life, Melissa. A fan of almost all things Sci-Fi and Horror, he is a devout reader of Jeremy Robinson, Jeff Strand, Brian Keene, and Tim Curran; their work has been a large influence on him. These are in addition to horror greats like H.P. Lovecraft and Stephen King.

www.ingramcontent.com/pod-product-compliance
Lightning Source LLC
Chambersburg PA
CBHW020633130626
46552CB00003B/1210